MYSTERIES IN OUR NATIONAL PARKS

MYSTERY
#12

MYSTERIES
IN OUR NATIONAL PARKS

Buried Alive

GLORIA SKURZYNSKI AND ALANE FERGUSON

NATIONAL GEOGRAPHIC SOCIETY

WASHINGTON, D.C.

From Lanie to my husband, Ron,
who has given me the adventure of a lifetime.

Map by Carl Mehler, Director of Maps
Map research and production by Matt Chwastyk, Joseph F. Ochlak,
and Martin S. Walz

This is a work of fiction. Any resemblance to living persons or events other
than descriptions of natural phenomena is purely coincidental.

Library of Congress Cataloging-in-Publication Data
has been requested.

3 9082 09271 4560

Printed in the United States of America

ACKNOWLEDGMENTS

The authors are grateful to so many people at
Denali National Park who helped in the creation of this
book: Joe Van Horn, Wilderness Coordinator;
Diane Brown, Communication Center Manager;
Stacey Chadwick, Staff Assistant to Superintendent;
Theresa Philbrick, Staff Assistant to Interpretation;
Martha Tomeo, Education Specialist; Clare Curtis,
Supervisory Park Ranger; Annalie Wright, Park Ranger
Protection; Stan Steck, Park Pilot; Doug Stockdale, Public
Information Officer; Tom Habecker, Park Ranger;
Pat Owen, Wildlife Biologist; Amanda Austin, Biological
Science Technician; Chelsie Venechuk, Cultural Resource
Technician; Carmen Adamyk, Kennels Assistant;
Karen Fortier, Kennels Manager; Paul Anderson,
Superintendent; Diane Chung, Deputy Superintendent. A
very special thanks to Beth Van Couwenberghe for her
generosity in hosting us at McKinley Village Lodge.

DENALI
NATIONAL
PRESERVE

N

Tonzona River

DENALI
NATIONAL
PRESERVE

DENALI NATIONAL PARK AND PRESERVE

STATE: Alaska

ESTABLISHED: 1917 as Mount McKinley National Park; 1980 enlarged and renamed Denali National Park and Preserve

AREA: 6 million acres (larger than the state of Massachusetts)

NAME: "Denali" means "high one" in the language of the Athapascan people; McKinley honors William McKinley, 25th President of the United States.

NATURAL FEATURES: Permanent snowfields cover most of Mount McKinley (Denali), highest summit in North America, which towers over the jagged peaks of the Alaska Range. Evergreen forests called taiga give way to tundra, vast treeless meadows of dwarf plants and mosses that carpet the glacially carved valleys and mountainsides. More than 150 varieties of birds, 751 types of plants, and 37 kinds of mammals thrive in this subarctic wonderland.

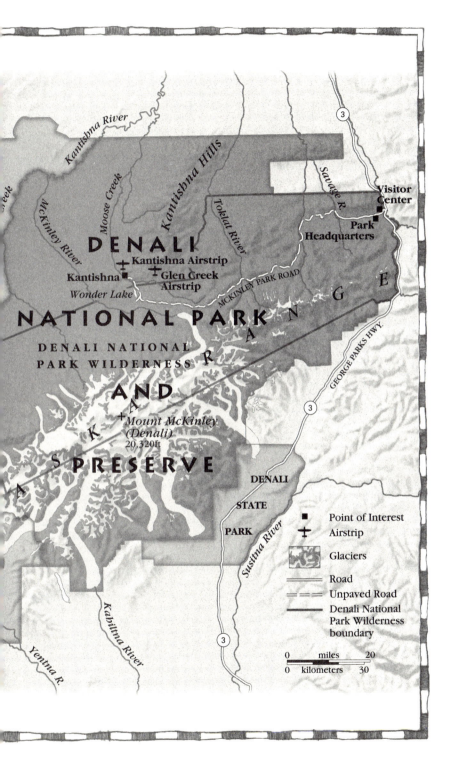

"I already told you, I'll take care of it!" the man barked. He took a final drag from his cigarette and crushed it in the ashtray so hard the tip splayed like a firecracker. "It's bad when the mark is a kid. Yeah, yeah, I know it's business, but I'm telling you, this is it, just one more time. You're costing me, man. I had my own game going, and now I'll have to end it. After this job, I'm through—you got that? Through. Do your own dirty work."

Slamming the phone into its cradle, he stared out the window at the setting sun. It was low in the west, and it edged the clouds with a ring of brilliant gold. So they'd found him. He'd come all the way to Alaska to get away from his old life, but the hooks ran deep. Even in the vast wilderness, he couldn't disappear, not from them. Well, after this job, he'd take his money and leave. This time he'd go to Mexico. There was a chance he could really vanish in Mexico.

The man walked to a drawer and opened it. Carefully, he pulled out a nickel-plated revolver and rubbed it on his sleeve until the light played along the barrel like a liquid bead. Then he jammed it into his belt and shrugged on his jacket. They'd told him this would be it. They said they'd never call him again. So what if it was a kid? He had a job to do.

Just one more time.

CHAPTER ONE

The lights of the aurora borealis flashed across the Alaskan sky in sheets of color: bright, dancing curtains of pale green and crimson that took Jack's breath away. Every few seconds the aurora shimmered with new brilliance, its hues shifting from incandescent greens to soft pinks to blues to luminous white, as though a giant kaleidoscope had been set among the stars. He stood in awe in Denali's frigid stillness. There was no way he could capture this with his simple camera, no way to reduce this magic onto photo paper. It was as if he were watching the heavens being painted by the hand of God.

"Awhooo!" Thirteen-year-old Nicky Milano, the Landons' newest temporary foster child, threw back his head and howled at the northern lights. His breath made a steady stream of frost as he danced backward on his left leg, his right boot pumping the air furiously when

he hopped along the pristine snow. "I'm seeing it, I'm feeling it, I'm loving it, I'm digging it," he cried while somehow managing to shift his backside beneath his parka. "Oh yeah. *Yip, yip, yip, awhoooo!*"

Ashley, Jack's 11-year-old sister, doubled over with laughter, but Jack could only shake his head in disbelief. His parents stood less than 20 feet away, too engrossed in setting up a photograph to do more than give Nicky a quick nod. Steven Landon struggled with a tripod, while Olivia held her husband's expensive wide-angle camera close to her chest, careful not to drop it in the snow.

"Awhooo."

"Nicky, what the *heck* are you doing, anyway?" Jack demanded.

"Howling!" Nicky cried. He stopped dancing and turned to Jack, cinching his hood tight. With the hood pulled almost to the bridge of his nose and his stiff parka collar zipped up so far it skimmed the bottom of his ears, Nicky's face had been reduced to the size of a fist. Jack could no longer see Nicky's slicked-back copper hair and the real diamond stud that pierced his right ear, but he could still hear his wise-guy accent. Nicky sounded as though he should be prowling the streets of New York instead of the wilds of Denali National Park in Alaska.

"I heard that true Alaskans bay like wolves when they see the northern lights" Nicky explained. "I'm trying to be—you know—authentic. Yo, Ashley, why don't you give it a try?"

Ashley threw back her head and let loose a thin, high-pitched yowl. The jingle bells on her hat rang merrily as she tipped her head farther back, wailing at the flashing night sky. Jack had to laugh. She sounded more like a coyote.

"Do it, Jack," Ashley begged.

Shaking his head again, Jack said, "No thanks. You guys are completely crazy."

"Yeah?" Nicky clapped his gloved hands together to warm them. They made cracking sounds that echoed across the tundra like gunshots. "You think so?" When he smiled, his teeth flashed white in the half light. "You're right, Jack, I am crazy. And what's scary is, you don't know how crazy I can be. You have no idea *what* you're dealing with."

What did *that* mean, Jack wondered. Problem was, he'd probably never find out, because secrets swirled around Nicky Milano. And no one, not his mother or his father or Nicky himself, was talking.

The strangeness had begun three days ago in the Landon kitchen. Jack had just finished pouring a bowl of Cheerios and Ashley had taken a huge bite of an apple-cinnamon bagel when his parents slipped into the two remaining kitchen chairs, coffee cups in hand. Sunlight caught the blond stubble sprinkled across his father's chin like grains of sand. Watching him, Jack fingered the pale hairs that had sprouted beneath his own chin, but his were soft, thread-like. Still, those hairs might just grow into something. A goatee, maybe. He took a spoonful of cereal and waited for one of his parents to speak. He could tell they had something to say.

"Kids, we need to talk. There's a new foster child we've decided to accept," his father began. "His name is Nicky Milano, and he'll be going with us on our trip to Denali." Steven held up his hand to silence Jack's instant stream of objections. "I know it's last minute, but this is a very special case. Ms. Lopez asked us to take him as a favor, and we can't turn her down."

"Dad, we *can't* change things now!" Jack had protested. "Mom—" He'd looked to his mother for help. She'd just gotten out of the shower, and her long, black hair was already curling into soft rings that bounced as she shook her head.

"I'm afraid it's already settled," Olivia told him.

"But what about the wolverines? The park's counting on you to help find out why they're dying!"

"Don't worry about me. I can manage my job with an extra child in tow."

"But—"

"Sweetheart, I said I can manage."

A wildlife veterinarian, Olivia had received an emergency call from Denali National Park. A month earlier, a wolverine had been discovered dead inside the park boundaries. A week later, a second wolverine body had been found, again with no visible signs of trauma, and days later, yet another. Then, less than a week ago, two more wolverine bodies had been discovered in the same general area in the middle of Denali Wilderness. Park officials were mystified and alarmed. Wolverines were mysterious animals, so elusive they haunted the wilderness like ghosts. Most of the rangers had never even seen a wolverine in the wild. Now five had been discovered dead in less than a month! When they'd found no bullet holes, no apparent disease—nothing to explain why the animals had died—they'd turned to Olivia for help, as parks often did when they had a mystery involving animals.

In addition to the phone call from the park staff asking Olivia to investigate the deaths, she'd also heard from Chaz Green, the founder of the Wolverine Rescue Program. "You're an expert," he'd told Olivia. "We need you to solve this mystery. Please come, Dr. Landon, and help save the wolverines."

Now Jack took a breath and said, "I know you can do your job, Mom, but you told me this was the weirdest case you'd ever been called on. This Nicky kid will just get in the way."

Answering softly, Olivia replied, "Of course I realize it's bad timing, but the child has nowhere else to go. He used to live with his father but now his dad is…" There was a beat, and then the word, "…gone. His mom died in an accident when Nicky was six. He has no other relatives. He's alone, Jack."

Jack placed his feet on the chair rungs and slouched down, his hand pushing the ball of his cheek almost into his eye. Ashley kept chewing on her bagel as if having Nicky join them didn't bother her in the slightest. That was like her. His sister never seemed to mind when new people burst into their lives and flipped everything upside down, but it drove Jack crazy. Foster kids were always a gamble. Since his dad had been a foster child himself when he was young, Steven welcomed any child in need, wanting to "put something back into the system," as he put it. Olivia often said she would love to take in kids full-time, but because of her intense schedule she would have to settle for offering temporary care. Temporary was plenty for Jack.

"Don't worry about our Denali trip, Son, it'll be just as good," Steven said, reaching over to touch Jack's shoulder. "We still get to stay in a ranger's house near park headquarters, and we'll still get to see all kinds of cool animals. Nothing will change."

Jack sighed loudly. "OK, I'm sure it'll all be great." Forcing a smile, he tried to look like he meant it. It was selfish not to want to help someone in need. He just required a little time to get used to the idea. He pushed the Cheerios around his bowl until milk splashed on the tabletop and his dad told him to stop before he made a mess.

Ashley, her mouth full of bagel, asked, "So what happened to the dad?"

That was when Jack first sensed that there was something odd about Nicky's situation. For a moment, neither one of his parents said a word. Olivia picked up a spoon and began stirring her coffee, but she hadn't put any cream or sugar in it. *Clink, clink, clink*—the spoon tapped against the sides of the mug. She and Steven exchanged glances.

"What's wrong?" Ashley asked again, wide eyed. "Is his dad dead, too?"

"Nicky's father is still alive. I—" Olivia cleared her throat. "Well, actually, we, can't go into detail. Ms. Lopez and the Department of Social Services said it was essential to keep everything about Nicky quiet. His background is...confidential."

For a minute, Jack didn't know what to say. Were his parents refusing to tell them about a foster kid who would be sharing their lives for who knew how long? What was up with that? Jack finally let out a snort, saying, "You're kidding, right?"

"I'm afraid not." Olivia took another sip of coffee and met his gaze head-on. Her eyes were dark and round, the same as Ashley's. Jack's were blue like his father's.

"Why can't you say anything? Is Nicky dangerous?"

"Of course not."

"Is he a nut case?" This from Ashley.

Setting her mug down hard, Olivia said, *"No!* And I would appreciate it if you didn't talk like that."

Ashley tried a different approach. "So…we're not supposed to bug him, but if he tells us about his life, then that's OK, right?"

"He can't," Steven answered. "I mean, he won't. Look, it's a complicated situation. Nicky'll only be with us a short while, and during that time you are not to pry." He rubbed the back of his neck while he talked, a sure sign that he was worrying about something. "Of course you can chat with him all you want, just don't…"

"…poke around in his past," Olivia finished at a gallop. "Understand?"

"Yep." Ashley nodded but added, "That's really strange, though." Her hair hadn't been brushed yet, so it stood out from her head in dark, fuzzy corkscrews. A too-big blue terry cloth robe drooped crazily off of one shoulder, and her slippers made her feet seem even bigger than they were, like a puppy's oversize paws. She looked at Jack and wiggled her eyebrows. "Nicky Milano, man of mystery. I think our trip to Alaska is going to be *very* interesting."

Jack thought about that conversation now as Nicky's eyes flashed in the spangle of the northern lights. Man of mystery was right. They'd been together for more than 24 hours, and Jack still didn't know a thing about Nicky, not really. Nicky talked, but he didn't say anything, as if his true thoughts were kept locked inside out of reach. The most he'd actually admitted about himself was that he was crazy. Well, maybe he was.

"Mom, Dad, everyone—look over there!" Ashley cried excitedly, pointing into the distance. "Something's moving. Way off, where it's flat. Look, Nicky, it's right there." She leaned close to him, so that their heads touched. "See that stand of trees? Now, go to your left. It's in that open space."

Nicky followed Ashley's finger and nodded. "Yeah, yeah, I see it. What is it?"

"I can't tell for sure—it's too dark."

Glittering snow stretched out before them like a sheet, and in the distance Jack could see an ink-black shape that seemed the size of a half dollar. With fingers made clumsy by gloves, Jack pulled out his camera. It took him a moment to locate the figure in his viewfinder, but when he finally did and focused the zoom lens, he knew immediately what it was. The animal seemed to stagger in the snow, bending down on one knee before rising up on unsteady legs. A few steps later it stumbled again.

"It's a deer," Jack announced.

"Caribou," Olivia corrected.

"But it doesn't have any antlers."

"That's because they dropped off last fall. If you were close enough, you'd see tiny little buds on the top of his head. Those buds are the beginnings of his new antlers. By June he'll have a big, branching rack. Just think of how much growth that is in three short months!"

Puzzled, Ashley asked, "But where's the rest of the herd? I thought caribou traveled together."

"They usually do," Olivia replied, "but it's not too uncommon for one to be traveling alone." She placed Steven's camera to her eye, twisting the powerful zoom lens to enlarge the image. "Oh, no, I see what's wrong. He's injured. The others probably went on ahead of him. This guy couldn't keep up."

Ashley wailed, "Can't you help him, Mom?"

"I can't, honey." Olivia quickly explained that Denali National Park wouldn't allow her to interfere and that part of what makes national parks so special is that natural processes are allowed to happen. This means injured animals are never helped. "I'm sorry, Ashley. That's just the way nature works."

Steven said, "Better give me back my camera, Olivia. It's time we started packing. We have to fly to Kantishna in the morning, and it's already been a long day."

Ashley stood next to Nicky. From the way her eyebrows crunched together, Jack could tell she felt upset about the caribou. Of course Jack felt bad about it, too, but what really preoccupied him was what Nicky had said. "You don't know what you're dealing with." Was he joking, or giving a warning?

Jack was just placing his own camera in his case when he heard it—a thin, wailing cry that hung in the air like a single, haunting note. First low, then high, it rang across the frozen space until a second, then a third voice joined in an eerie choir. From his time in Yellowstone, Jack recognized the cry of a wolf.

"It sounds like wolves!" Olivia said, her voice filled with excitement. "That would be an amazing thing to witness on our first night in Denali."

Jack pulled out his camera again to zoom in on the caribou. "I can't tell for sure, but I think the wolves are behind the trees. I see some movement—yeah! Here they come!"

Dark liquid shapes bolted out from the spruce trees, advancing quickly toward the injured animal. Jack counted six. They were moving in tandem, cutting in and out in a strange pattern, first three and three, then four and two. In a panic, the caribou tried to run but became encircled by the quicksilver shadows. It was both gruesome and awesome, this dance of death. The caribou made it only a few steps before a shadow cut it off. Switching directions, it stumbled and then, lightning quick, a wolf pounced, grabbing the caribou by the throat.

"I can't stand it," Ashley cried.

"It's OK," Nicky told her. "Just don't look."

It was over as quickly as it began. The rest of the wolves surrounded the kill, ripping pieces of its hide as if it were tissue paper. Ashley dropped her face into her hands.

"Sweetheart, you know that the wolves have to eat to stay alive," Steven told her gently. "It's the circle of life. There's an old saying: Nothing in nature offends nature. This is elimination of the weak, survival of the fittest."

Olivia rubbed Ashley's back between her shoulder blades, her glove making a slipping sound against the parka. "The mother wolves will be having babies in the first part of May. The females need to eat for their pups. You wouldn't want the wolves to starve, would you? Just think of the little wolf pups."

"I know, I know, but...the caribou is still dead."

No one knew how to answer that. Finally, Nicky spoke, his voice both deep and quiet. "I know what it's like to be left behind. I know what it's like to be ripped to pieces. No one should ever get used to it."

With that, he turned and walked toward the Jeep.

CHAPTER TWO

"**J**ack, wake *up*," Ashley hissed in his ear. Her hands clamped onto his shoulder, and she rocked him so hard his teeth chattered. "There's a moose outside in the back woods. She's huge! I've never seen such long, spindly legs. It's amazing. Come on!"

"What—what time is it?" Jack asked groggily. It was way too early for this much chatter.

"Six fifty-seven in the morning, which means it's really 8:57 Jackson Hole time. Get up, lazy bum."

Jack tried to open his eyes, but his lids refused to cooperate. He'd had a hard time sleeping in the ranger family's house, probably because he kept hearing sounds all night. Since most hotels that served the park were closed until mid-May, the Landons had relied on the generosity of the park for a place to stay during this first week of April. It had been a real stroke of luck that one of the ranger families was spending some time in Utah, so they'd offered the Landons their home while they were away. Their house was furnished with three bedrooms on the main floor and one in the basement, plus a living room, two bathrooms, and a small, sunny kitchen. Nicky had asked for the room in the basement, which gave Jack and Ashley, in addition to their parents, rooms of their own. Perfect, except that the mysterious night noises had kept Jack restless. The digital clock had registered 3:42 before he finally figured out that the thuds were nothing but clumps of snow sliding off the pitched roof.

"Must...sleep," Jack groaned now, hugging his pillow over his ears.

He saw a streak of yellow light as his sister yanked the pillow away from his face, but he jerked it back harder, practically smashing his nose into his face.

"Don't be such a weenie." Ashley's words were muffled by the pillow. One by one, she tried to pry away his fingers.

Jack clamped his pillow in a death grip. "Show the moose to Nicky," he croaked.

"I knocked, but he didn't answer. I can't just go into his room. What if he doesn't wear pajamas?"

Pulling the pillow off his face, Jack tried to focus. His sister's cheeks and nose had pinked up from the cold, and her hair billowed out from the bottom of her hat in an inverted mushroom cloud. She had on a pair of jeans and an unzipped parka with a single glove shoved in each pocket. Underneath she wore a blue nightshirt spangled with moons and stars, which hung loosely over her jeans to her knees. The tongues of her boots stuck out, and the laces dragged against the floor like whiskers. In her odd getup, she looked like a cartoon.

He could hear his sister stomp her foot. "Hurry up!"

"Go *away!*" Jack moaned.

"OK, fine. Miss the moose."

Her footsteps clomped on the wooden floor as she flounced off, and then Jack heard the creak of an outside door. He lay there for a minute, then flipped the covers off and rolled out the rest of the way. He rubbed his eyes with the heels of his hands, but it was no use fighting it. He was awake. Well, he sighed, he might as well see the animal that cost him an extra hour of sleep. Grabbing his parka and camera, he stepped into his sneakers, not bothering to search for his socks. Then he entered the dim hallway.

It had surprised Jack, the way all the Denali ranger homes looked exactly like regular run-of-the-mill houses. He'd been expecting a split-log cabin heated by a wood-burning stove and maybe an old-fashioned hand pump for water. In his mind he'd pictured an outhouse behind every porch. Instead, this house and all the others in the cluster looked just like the tract homes in Jackson Hole. Indoor plumbing and everything.

Once outside, he followed his sister's footprints to the back of the house. It had snowed hard in the middle of the night, a deep, fluffy layer of white that mounded on the branches like dollops of whipped cream. Light snow kicked into his shoes and onto bare skin, so he tried to walk in Ashley's boot prints. When that didn't work, he switched to threading a path inches from the side of the house, where the snow was still packed. He found Ashley hunched behind a spruce tree. When she turned and saw him, she smiled, then placed her finger to her lips and pointed to a cluster of trees.

A huge moose munched lazily on bare twigs, its large, bulbous nose and neck bell bobbing with every bite. Jack held his breath as the moose moved forward, crunching through the trees until it was less than ten feet away. Although he knew the powerful animal could be dangerous, he couldn't pass on what could be the best shot of his life. Carefully, he unzipped his camera case and was just raising his camera to his face when he heard a door squeak noisily from the screened-in porch on the south end of the house. The moose snapped its head up and looked in the direction of the noise. Jack froze, until the moose dropped its head to begin eating again.

"...thought I'd come out here for a cup of coffee, even though it's a bit nippy. I wanted to talk to you about the wolverines." Two chairs scraped noisily across the wooden planks. His parents wouldn't be able to see the moose from the porch.

"This is the strangest case I've ever been called on. I'm hoping this cold air will clear my head so I can think it through. There's something about these deaths that just doesn't add up."

"Like what?" Steven asked.

Jack could hear his mother sigh. "First of all, I've read through stacks of papers, and the truth is no one really knows much about this animal. They're still very mysterious. And it doesn't help that they are surrounded by myths and legends. There's one story where a wolverine supposedly broke into a cabin and ate a trapper alive."

"Ouch!"

"Steven, you know that's utter nonsense."

His parents' voices distracted Jack. He didn't want to hear about wolverines when he had a huge moose in his camera's viewfinder. He wished they'd keep quiet so they wouldn't scare away this animal before Jack got some pictures. Compared with all the pictures of moose he'd seen in books, this one looked twice as big, maybe because he was so close to it.

The moose took another mouthful of twigs and munched idly, although Jack thought it might be watching him. He'd heard that more people got hurt from moose than from grizzlies, so he didn't want to tick this big guy off. Just keep it nice and easy, he told himself. Zooming in so close he could count its eyelashes, he began to snap photos.

Ashley huddled beneath the tree branches like a turtle in a shell, watching the animal with rapt attention. "We should get Mom and Dad so they can see this," she whispered.

"No, don't move. I don't want to scare him. If he decides to charge us, we're toast."

The moose backed up, his enormous head whipping past branches as he turned to go. Even though he knew it wouldn't make a great picture, Jack snapped a few of the animal's rump.

"Maybe we should go tell Mom and Dad now," she suggested. "They can still get a look at it, even if it's moving away."

"Nah, don't bother. They're all hung up on the wolverine stuff." Jack didn't feel like sharing the moose experience with his parents—or more truthfully, with his father. He wanted to develop these pictures, and if they turned out as great as he thought they might, he'd present them to his dad as proof that he could take some spectacular shots too—even if he didn't have his dad's experience or his expensive camera equipment.

Once again his parents' voices penetrated his consciousness. Olivia was saying, "A wolverine would rather run away than fight anything its size or larger. If they hunt anything, it's usually ground squirrels. But lack of information is just one problem. The whole case has got me all turned around. For one thing,

I don't like the way those bodies were found."

"You mean because the last two were next to snow-mobile tracks?"

"Exactly. It doesn't make sense, Steven. They're such secretive animals, so why would they even come close to the trail? And *two* of them this last time…two males together? The fact is wolverine males are solitary. They keep to their own territories. I just don't get it."

"Were they hit by the snowmobiles?"

"The report says there are absolutely no signs of impact. The last two bodies are at Kantishna. I'll know more when I examine them, but it appears they weren't hit. It's just baffling."

Jack knew about the report. After they'd arrived in Anchorage, they'd driven directly to Denali, found the house they were to stay in, then quickly unpacked before heading to the ranger station, where his mother had been given a packet with pictures of the dead animals. Now he heard a rustling as his mother handed some papers to his father.

"…deaths are compounded by another sad statistic," she was saying. "This report says wolverine young have a very high mortality rate—up to 30 percent."

"From humans hunting them?" Steven asked.

"No. Unrelated adults appear to be killing the kits of other wolverines. But *30 percent!* That's a huge amount to lose. Which underscores how the wolver-ine population can't afford the loss of apparently healthy adults. They'll be in serious trouble if we don't get a handle on this."

"Nature can be cruel," he told her. "Although I must admit I've thought about eating my own young once or twice."

"Steven!"

He just laughed. A beat later he said, "I still think nature can't hold a candle to the viciousness of the human race. Look at Nicky's situation."

Olivia dropped her voice low. "Seriously, what could be more savage than that? The whole thing makes me sick."

Jack and Ashley exchanged glances. Both of them knew they weren't supposed to be hearing this. Every time they asked about Nicky, they were told his life was "confidential." Yet here was a chance for them to find out something—maybe just a little. After all, they were the ones who had to put up with Nicky Milano, man of mystery.

"It's true—those people have ice in their veins," Steven was saying. "They have no conscience. All things considered, I think taking Nicky was for the best."

Ashley had begun to creep forward so she could hear better, but Jack grabbed her by the arm. Any motion might alert their parents, who would be really angry if they caught the two of them eavesdropping.

"I agree, but I have to admit I'm still worried," Olivia continued. "What about Ashley and Jack? When it's all said and done, they are our first priority. Are you sure they'll be safe?"

"Olivia, we're in Denali, thousands of miles from any kind of danger," Steven insisted. "No one could possibly find us here. Who would even think to look at a wildlife veterinarian and her photographer husband up here in the frozen north? You're worrying over nothing."

"But what if?…" Olivia pressed.

"We can't live our lives for the 'what ifs.'"

"You're right, you're right. I'm also worried about Nicky. He's pleasant enough, but how much of all this does he actually understand?"

Jack felt his nerves tingle. The cold bit through the flimsy pajama flannel, numbing his legs. He was holding his breath, straining to catch every word when he heard it—the barely-there sound of footsteps in the snow, as soft as the wind rustling through trees. He turned, nearly jumping out of his skin until he realized it was Nicky wearing a knit ski hat pulled down over his face, with holes for the eyes and mouth. It made him look creepy, like he was going to rob a 7-Eleven or something.

"Naughty, naughty," Nicky whispered, pointing to the two of them and then to Steven and Olivia.

Jack's body froze, but his cheeks flushed with embarrassment. Caught in the act by Nicky!

Nicky put his finger to his lips and motioned for them to follow him. Ashley crept forward, pulling Jack's gloved hand; he fell in behind the two retreating figures, moving through the snow this time, not caring how cold his feet got. Had Nicky heard what his parents had been saying? How long had he been standing there spying on them?

The sun was brighter now, making latticework shadows against the glittering whiteness. Nicky kept walking, past a stand of conifers and a boulder with a surface scored like elephant skin, along a tamped-down pathway that led to the corner of the yard, over to a small wooden picnic table where he swept the snow off the wooden bench and pointed for them to sit down. He had on all his gear—parka, boots and gloves, and that weird knit ski mask, blood red in color, that covered his face all the way down to his neck.

"You think we can talk, you know, in private out here?" he asked softly. "We could go inside, but I've been taught to say what I have to say in open spaces. You OK with that?"

When Ashley nodded, Nicky said, good, because it was important that no one else hear what he had to tell them. Since he seemed to be waiting for Jack to comment, Jack asked, "How long were you standing there behind me and Ashley?"

"Long enough. I went outside early—I saw a moose. Did you catch that bull moose, Ashley? It was standing over there by the back fence, where the rail is split."

"Yes." Ashley nodded. "Yes, I did. But I thought it was a girl."

"Nope. It had that bell thingy hanging down from its neck, which makes it a guy. I read it in a book."

Jack felt his impatience rising as Nicky smiled a little, his lips visible through the lower hole of the ski mask. Was he just playing games Jack wondered? You'd think you'd be able to read a person's expression as long as the eyes and mouth showed, but it didn't work that way, Jack realized. All parts of a face had to come together to project gloom or joy, fear or scorn, interest or mockery.

"Then I saw you two, and I said to myself, 'Nicky, something's going on. Someone is talking.'" Before Jack had a chance to answer, Nicky waved his hand and said, "Your parents should be more careful."

"Wait a minute. What do you mean they should be more careful?" Jack demanded. "We still didn't learn anything about this 'danger' we might be in. I want to know who you are and why exactly you're here with us."

"If I told you, I'd have to kill you."

Ashley caught her breath, but Nicky just laughed. "Come on guys, that was a joke. I'm trying to lighten the mood here."

"I don't think you're funny," Jack told him.

Nicky's voice turned suddenly grave. "Yeah. Nothing much about my life has been funny. It actually sucks. But it's going to get better. My dad—he promised me that." He looked out into the trees, his dark eyes staring at something Jack couldn't see.

It was Ashley who finally broke the silence. "Can you tell us?" she asked softly. When she spoke, her breath made a tiny cloud.

Nicky shifted on the bench. "I'm not supposed to. But then again, you went and heard, so maybe I can tell you some. I'm from Philadelphia—maybe you already know that. It was just me and my dad and then about a week ago…about a week ago he had to leave, and I had to find a place to land and that's how I ended up with you. But don't feel sorry for me or nothin'," he rushed on. "We're going to get back together soon, me and my dad, and then I'll be outta here. It's all good."

Jack scowled. Hadn't his parents said there was danger? Hadn't they talked about hiding from who-knew-what up in the frozen north? He wanted to reach out and shake Nicky, but Ashley kept talking in her calm voice, as if they were having a conversation about oatmeal. What was it like living in a big city? Crowded, Nicky answered, but with really good restaurants that served dishes with names he couldn't pronounce and spices that made his tongue burn and streets that were lit up like noon all night long and stayed bustling until the crack of dawn. What was his favorite class? Science, because you got to dissect real frogs. After that maybe math. For ten long minutes the conversation droned on, Nicky's dark eyes locked on Ashley's, his mouth seeming disconnected because of the ski mask, as if it belonged to a ventriloquist's dummy.

"…so I'm a city kid who ended up in the frozen north. Man, who'd a thought?" Nicky shook his head. "I can't believe they would send me all the way here. But that Ms. Lopez lady was right; I do feel OK about it. Except for maybe the wolves and bears." The whole time he'd been talking Nicky had been working on a tiny eight-inch snowman, and now he stuck two spruce needle arms on it as well as a spruce needle nose. "You like this thing?" he asked Ashley.

Jack's annoyance deepened. If his sister wanted to chatter like nothing was wrong, that was fine, but he was sick of pretending the three of them were rambling through a regular conversation. Whatever Nicky's secret was, Jack wanted to know and he wanted to know now. "What are you running away from?" he demanded.

The smile faded from Nicky's face.

"You heard what my parents said—that no one would think to look at a wildlife veterinarian and all of that. So who's looking?"

No answer.

"If you're not going to tell us, then why'd you bring us over to this table?"

No answer.

"I mean, why all the secrets? Why don't you just tell us and then we can go into the house and have some hot chocolate and forget about it. This is just dumb."

Nicky held up his right hand. "No, it's all right," he said to Ashley when she began to argue that Nicky should be able to tell things the way he wanted to. "Jack's right. See, that's the part I need you guys to understand." His voice became suddenly slow, deliberate, and in an odd way everything around them seemed to hush. Even a black-billed magpie that had been fluttering at the top of a spruce stopped its strident cawing. "There are…things…about me…you need to leave alone. Not that I don't want to tell you, but it's not safe for you to know."

Snorting, Jack said, "Oh, come on, get real. You're in Alaska. Nobody's going to find you up here. Mom and Dad said so."

"I'm not talking about me." He cocked his fingers as if he were holding a gun, and pointed at the snowman. He pretended to shoot, then blew at the tip of his finger as if clearing smoke from a gun barrel. "I'm talking about you two."

"Yeah, yeah," Jack scoffed. "Somebody's gonna come all the way up here to shoot us. Who? A terrorist?"

Nicky's eyes narrowed, and he breathed quickly once or twice, sending vapor into the cold air. Jack could almost see the wheels turning inside his head as he thought things over. Suddenly he said, "I can't really break my oath of secrecy, but we'll play a guessing game. About my dad, right? I'll give you a clue, and you have to figure it out." His eyes were still narrowed, but now they had a glint in them.

"A game," Jack said. "OK. Go."

"Here's the clue," Nicky announced. "Charlie is alive."

"Who's Charlie?" Ashley asked.

"That's the clue. You have to guess." Nicky set the little snowman in the center of the table and pretended to shoot it, using his finger as a gun.

"Is the snowman Charlie?" Jack wanted to know.

"No. The snowman is dead. Charlie is the clue. Charlie. Is. Alive." As Nicky bit off each word, Ashley looked toward Jack and shrugged.

Jack swept his gaze around the snowy landscape. "I got it," he said. "Charlie is the magpie up there in the tree. It's still alive."

Nicky shook his head. "You guys are so dense. Charlie's no one. Charlie is just a word. OK, I'll give you another clue. Can icicles attack?"

"Huh?" What kind of clue was that? Jack strained his imagination to come up with some solution to the puzzle, because he couldn't let Nicky beat him in this little brain game. He no longer cared whether it would reveal anything about Nicky's father; it was just that he needed to win, to silence that superior tone in Nicky's voice. Two clues, he told himself. *Charlie is alive. Can icicles attack?* "Well," he muttered, "each sentence has three words."

Ashley grew excited and added, "And the three words start with the same letters."

"C-I-A!" Jack yelled. "Your dad's with the CIA."

Nicky leaped forward, slamming his hand over Jack's mouth. "Keep it quiet," he hissed. "Keep it quiet."

CHAPTER THREE

Jack looked out the window of the plane and let the scenery wash thoughts of Nicky out of his mind. Beneath him was the frozen Toklat River, a winding, silver-white braid lacing through mountains that looked like sleeping dragons. Having traced the thin spider vein of the Toklat along his map, he knew it would flow out of the Alaska Range to join the Kantishna River, which would eventually flow into the Tanana River then to the mighty Yukon, which emptied into the Bering Sea. But the scene below couldn't be translated by the ink scribbles on his map; this park was too immense, too beautiful, too vast. At six million acres, Denali National Park and Preserve covered three times the area of Yellowstone, and here there were no highways threaded with bumper-to-bumper traffic; no miles of walkway criss-crossing the forest like scattered pick-up sticks.

The wilderness beneath him was an untouched pattern of tundra and kettle ponds and spruce forests. His mother had told him that parts of this landscape had never felt the tread of a human foot, and that knowledge made Jack glad. In a way it took the edge off the uneasiness he'd been feeling about Nicky.

Ever since Nicky had pointed his finger to pretend-shoot the snowman, Jack's distrust of him had grown. Saying that he couldn't tell Jack and Ashley about his life or they'd be in danger—how phony it all sounded! Of course the version Nicky told did tie in a little bit with what Jack's parents had said—that up in Alaska they were "thousands of miles away from any kind of danger." And yet he had to be faking it. Vows of silence? That stuff about the CIA? What was that all about? Jack wished his folks would just tell the whole story straight up so he could figure out what was going on. Instead, he was forced to make sense from whatever scraps of information he could stitch together, a line here and a bit there, like tiny patches on a quilt.

Pressing his forehead against the small window, he felt the plane's vibration run straight through his skull and into his jaw. In an odd way it felt good because something else was bothering him. He wasn't quite sure how to put words onto it. Maybe if the throb of the engine filled his head, he wouldn't have to think.

He watched the mountains unroll below in a rhythm of peaks and valleys, the tops of them treeless and bare, the valleys empty sugar bowls of snow. From his books he knew that the summer would bring wildflower carpets and willow thickets that hid 37 species of mammals. Concentrate on those, he commanded his brain. Instead, his mind kept flashing back to Nicky, and he realized what else was gnawing at him. It was Ashley. When they'd sat at the picnic table, her wide-set eyes had watched Nicky's every move in a way he'd never seen before. Jack didn't like it. He didn't like the way her face lit up when Nicky talked about his life. He especially didn't like the way she swallowed Nicky's every word, gulping down his story like a baby bird. Yeah, exactly like a baby bird. In his mind he hatched a picture of her with a beak-mouth opened wide as Nicky fed her one fantasy after another.

Nicky had finished up by saying, "Remember, keep all this a secret. I'm trusting you guys. Spies are everywhere. I mean the bad guys."

"You can count on us," Ashley had breathed. "You have our promise. We will not tell a word to Mom or Dad or anyone. No one will ever know that we know. Right, Jack? *Right, Jack?*"

Jack had stood there, brushing the snow off his pajama bottoms, muttering, "Sure, right."

He hadn't believed a word of it. But he was curious. How could he tease the truth from his parents, or from Nicky?

"Gorgeous enough for you?" Olivia asked loudly.

She'd been busy chatting about wolverines with the ranger directly across from her while Jack had drifted inside his own thoughts. Now his mother's voice snapped him back.

"Yeah. Pretty amazing," he answered.

Since they were flying to Kantishna airstrip in a bush plane, the engine's roar drowned out anything said in a normal voice. Jack, Olivia, a ranger named Blake Van Horn, and the pilot, Eric, were in this plane, while Nicky, Ashley, Steven, and another ranger/pilot flew behind them in a second plane.

"They call Alaska the last frontier, and it certainly is that. Look!" Olivia's arm brushed against Jack as she pointed out the small window. "Not a single person as far as the eye can see." Her arm flew back as she clutched her seat and said, "Whoa—the air's getting rough. I hope Ashley's OK in the other plane. You know how queasy she gets from turbulence."

Jack bet Ashley's skin would be blanched as white as the snow beneath them—white with a green tinge, since she really hated being bumped around in small planes. Well, if she got sick, at least Jack wouldn't be there to see it. Maybe she could throw up on Nicky. The thought made him smile. He reached out to steady himself as the plane bounced even harder.

"Sorry! These little planes can be a bit of a roller-coaster ride," Blake told them.

Leaning forward so he could see Blake better, Jack

said, "Mom told me you were the one who found the last two wolverine bodies."

"Yep. I was the first ranger on the scene, although the actual call came from Chaz Green from the Wolverine Rescue Program. He had his dogsled out by Kantishna when he discovered the bodies, and he called us immediately. When I mushed out I found two dead male wolverines only a few feet apart. So weird. You talked to Chaz, didn't you, Olivia?"

"Yes. He called me in Jackson Hole and told me what he knew. He was really helpful—and very passionate about the wolverines. I went to his Web site and was truly impressed."

"He sure wants to protect those critters," Blake agreed. "I wish there were more people like him." Blake was tall and muscular, with deep-set eyes the same flinty gray as his hair, which curled over his collar like a baby's fingers. He had a well-trimmed beard, something Jack wasn't used to in park rangers. Most of the ones Jack had met were clean-shaven. The skin on Blake's face and hands had been burned a leathery brown-red, and deep lines ran from the corners of his eyes all the way to his ears, like tiny curtain pleats. He was the type of ranger who looked as tough as the land he patrolled.

"Chaz is the guy taking us mushing, right?" Jack asked.

"That's right." Olivia nodded. "He volunteered to

take you kids on a sled dog expedition while I'm examining the wolverine bodies."

"You ever been mushing, Jack?" Blake asked.

Jack shook his head. "This'll be my first time."

"Oh, you'll love it." Reaching beneath his seat, Blake pulled out a small water bottle, snapped the plastic ring with a quick motion, then raised it to his lips. After a few swallows he added, "The dogs love it, too—they're bred for the job. You glide over that glassy tundra so fast you'll swear you're flying. I used to run the sled dog team at Denali kennels, and I've mushed the area to Wonder Lake many a time, just me and the dogs and nature. Nothing's better."

"I have a question," Jack began. He'd been around enough park rangers to know that most came in two types: the quiet ones, and the ones who were natural-born teachers. Blake was in the second category, hands down.

"OK," Blake grinned. "I'm ready. Shoot."

"How come the park still uses dogsleds instead of snowmobiles? I mean, Mom said there were snowmobile tracks by the wolverine bodies, so it must be OK to use them in Denali, right?"

"Yes and no," Blake answered. "It's complicated. There's Denali Wilderness, the additions to the National Park that we got in 1980, and the National Preserve. Snow machining is allowed in the park additions, where the dead wolverines were found."

"But you rangers just use the dogsleds—"

"—and that seems an archaic way to get around the park," Blake finished for him. "Well, let's think about it a minute. First of all, snow machines depend on gasoline to power them. Our dogs need a few fat bars and a couple bites of snow when we're out on patrol, and then of course dog kibble and more water at night. Which do you think is gentler on the environment?"

Jack smiled. That was easy—the fat bars and mouthfuls of snow. Very biodegradable.

"A second reason is that our dogs don't bark when they're running, which means there's no noise pollution with our dog teams. Snow machines make an unholy racket. That's why they're outlawed in the wilderness area. Did you know," he asked, training his steel gray eyes on Jack, "that Denali is the only national park with a working sled dog team?"

"No. That's really cool."

"Darn right it is." Blake leaned forward eagerly and rested his water bottle on his knee. Now it seemed he was really warming up. "Denali's dogs are absolutely unique," he said. "Think about it. Snow machines have parts that break down or freeze up. They pollute. They're loud. Sled dogs are none of those things, which makes them a much better choice for our pristine backcountry." Wiggling his shaggy eyebrows, he added, "And in my opinion the dogs are a heck of a lot more fun. You can't cuddle up with a snow machine."

"How come you call them snow machines instead of snowmobiles?"

Blake shrugged. "Everyone up north calls them 'snow machines.' Can't tell you why. They're the same things as snowmobiles, though. Hey," he interrupted himself, "would you two like something to drink? I have a couple extra bottles of water."

Both Jack and Olivia shook their heads. "We have our own, thanks," Olivia told him. "Speaking of water, Blake, I had a question, too. How do you keep so many animals hydrated? I was sitting here doing the math, and I can't figure out how you manage it. Four quarts per day per dog times what," Olivia asked, squinting, "eight dogs? That's a whole lot of water."

Jack thought he knew the answer to this one. "They eat snow, like Blake said."

"I wish that was all it took," Blake replied. He twisted the cap back onto the water bottle and set it onto the floor. Right then they hit another pocket of air, making the bottle tip over and spin to the back of the plane like a top. "Ah, just leave it," Blake commanded when he saw that Jack was about to retrieve the bottle. He went on to tell them it took ten to fifteen gallons of snow to melt into one gallon of water. In the meantime, he would have to unpack the sled, bring in the harnesses to dry, and check the dogs' feet for cuts before finally feeding his animals. "There's a rule in the north, and that rule is Dogs Eat First. After taking care of all that and attending to a few more tasks, I get to eat."

Once again Jack thought how hard it was to be a ranger in the Park Service. Their jobs seemed both physically and mentally tough, and yet every ranger he'd ever met loved life in the parks. It almost seemed that being a ranger was a calling, a vocation, like choosing to be a priest or a missionary. Well, in a way, all rangers were missionaries. It was as if the wilderness was their church, the animals their congregation. He turned that thought over as their plane banked sharply to the left. They were about to land at Kantishna.

A low mountain emerged to the north, and at its base he noticed the frozen branch of Moose Creek glinting in the sun. Parallel to the creek ran an airstrip, one of the smallest Jack had ever seen. Brush lined both sides of it. Jack had never been nervous in a plane before, but there was a first time, he supposed, for everything. His stomach clamped as the small plane dipped toward the narrow runway.

When the plane nosed down, Jack squeezed his eyes shut until he felt a thud as the plane's skis touched snow, then settled into a long glide along the strip. It was then Jack opened his eyes and let out a breath he hadn't realized he was holding. The roar of the engines cut to a whine as they glided to the end of the runway.

"It's a bit primitive." Blake laughed as he unbuckled his seat belt, "But we haven't lost a ranger yet. You look a bit pale there, Jack. You OK?"

"I'm fine," Jack lied.

After the pilot, Eric, stopped the plane, Blake jumped out and put down a footstool for the rest of them to step on. After they were all safely on the ground, Eric steered the aircraft off the runway to make room for the second plane. Within five minutes, it landed smoothly and easily on the strip. Then Blake carried the footstool to that plane, getting it in place just before the door banged open.

First Steven emerged, followed by a female ranger Jack didn't know—she must have been the pilot. They quickly joined the knot of rangers and wolverine experts who had gathered around Olivia, shaking hands of introduction as though they were old friends. He heard Blake telling them about a NATIONAL GEOGRAPHIC article on wolverines in Finland; it said that one of the animals had built a cave underneath the frozen body of a sheep. "Food and shelter all in one," Blake joked. Everyone seemed to enjoy the story.

Jack drifted toward the doorway of the second plane, waiting for Ashley to exit. Finally he saw her one shoe hit the stool. The foot wavered a little. Then another foot planted itself right next to Ashley's, this one a size ten extra-wide black snow boot. Nicky was there, an inch from her side, standing so close to Ashley that a beam of light couldn't get between them. Worst of all, Nicky's arm was draped around Ashley's shoulders.

Jack wanted to leap up, grab that arm, and fling the

arm and its owner backward inside the plane. And then maybe punch him, too. Punch Nicky Milano's lights right out. He clamped his teeth together to keep from yelling, "Leave my sister alone!"

CHAPTER 4

Nicky took a careful step down and gently guided Ashley toward the ground. Her skin was tinged the same color as the clouds that were beginning to collect at the edge of the sky, and her mouth was clamped in a firm line. When she caught sight of Jack, she gave a feeble "Hey, Bro" followed by "I don't feel so good." Her hand hovered around her mouth as she gingerly stepped down from the stool onto the airstrip.

"Why didn't Dad stay with you?" Jack demanded.

"Because she told him she'd be fine," Nicky answered. Then, to Ashley, he murmured, "Come on, you just need some air. Breathe deep. Yeah, that's the way. You're gonna keep it all down. The secret is in the way you breathe."

Jack stared at them. He hadn't zipped up his coat, and the cold bit into him with icy stabs. It felt good.

Bitter air to kill the heat rising inside him. Nicky must have noticed the expression on Jack's face because his arm suddenly dropped to his side. "Hey, what's the matter with you?" he asked. "You look like you wanna hit somebody."

"Nothing's the matter with me," Jack snapped. "Ashley, come over here. I want to talk to you. *Alone!*" he added when Nicky began walking with her.

"Whoa, man, whatever you say." Nicky took a step back and held up his hands, palms forward.

With more force than he meant, Jack grabbed Ashley's elbow and steered her to the other side of the plane where they could have some privacy. As they passed the plane's tail, he smelled the faint, acrid odor of fuel. They circled to the other side, around a grimy brown rim of snow darkened by a mixture of spruce needles and dirt. Once hidden behind the plane, Jack whirled around to ask, "What was *that?*"

Ashley stared at him, wide-eyed. "What was what?"

"That…thing…with Nicky." He punched the air with his finger. "Back there. He had his arm around you."

"So?" A smile tugged at the corners of her lips. "I was sick."

"That's not what it looked like to me!"

"I almost puked, OK? Nicky was helping."

"Yeah, helping himself."

In an instant laughter exploded from his sister, a giant guffaw. "Are you *kidding?* I mean, you're not serious! You don't think—Jack, he was just being nice!"

"You're only 11," Jack sputtered, embarrassed because his sister wasn't taking him more seriously. He could feel the heat rise in his cheeks, could feel that he was coloring up. For some reason, that made him all the madder. "I don't like him. I don't trust him. And now you're—he's—"

Straightening, Ashley said, "I'm 11 and a *half*."

Jack snorted. He pulled his jacket tight around his chest. He didn't know what he'd expected to have happen because he hadn't thought it through that far. But one thing was for sure: He hadn't bargained on the look of merriment in his sister's eyes.

Ashley's dark hair hung down her back. She pulled it into a rope, then deftly twisted it into a coil and tucked it at the base of her neck. Pulling up her hood, she said, "You know what? You're being stupid." She jerked the strings together and tied them tightly underneath her chin. "And you want to know what else? You're wrong. I like Nicky. He's really, really nice, and he's smart, and he knows an awful lot about all the CIA stuff."

"He's been telling you that garbage again?"

"It's not garbage. It's real. You know what I noticed on the plane? Nicky sat right next to the window, and when the light hit it, his hair almost glowed."

Jack's mind flashed on Nicky's copper-colored hair, meticulously combed back from his face. "So? What about it?"

"It's dyed. He could tell I was looking, so he whispered that he had to change his appearance so that the spies wouldn't recognize him. His real hair is black. I could see just the tiniest beginnings of roots right along his part, so I know he's telling the truth. Can you believe he has to hide like that? I mean, wow." Her mouth made the shape of an *O*.

"Ashley, lots of kids dye their hair. A lot of them dye it green with blue dots. It doesn't prove anything."

"It does to me."

The indignation inside Jack suddenly spread to Ashley. He was about to tell her what he thought about Nicky and his bizarre story and the fact that she was taken in by it when he heard their father calling from the knot of rangers. Jack looked toward the direction of Steven's voice. He could see movement beyond the plane, just the feet of the rangers and his parents and Nicky, walking off in pairs or singly. From where he stood, the body of the plane blocked their torsos, creating a strange effect. It seemed as if he were watching the legs of a gigantic centipede.

"Jack, you've got to give Nicky a chance," Ashley stated. "Please? The thing is, I don't want to fight with you. I want to have fun on the dogsled trip, and it won't be fun if you're all mad. OK?"

Jack's eyes swung back to his sister. The color had returned to her skin, especially at the tip of her nose. He heard their names called out again, this time by their mother, and he realized there was nothing more to say because there was no time to say it. "I'm not mad," he stated flatly. "I'm…angry."

"Like there's a difference? So get over it." She gave Jack one of her sudden smiles, threading her arm through his. They began to walk toward the others. As she pulled him along, she told him what the ranger had shared on the plane, that the part they sat in on the dogsled was called a basket and that they would be able to see Denali from Wonder Lake and did he know that the name Denali was Athapascan and it meant the "high one?" As they tramped through the snow, Jack tried to make his face unreadable. Ashley could think what she liked, he argued inside his head. Nicky was lying. He could feel it. He was as sure of it as he was of the cold seeping in through his open coat.

The entire group was waiting for them at the northwest end of the airstrip, chatting beneath a small lean-to shelter made of some kind of rough-hewn fir. Steven waved Ashley toward him.

"How are you feeling, sweetheart?" he asked.

"Better."

"Good. Everyone, you've already met Nicky. This is our daughter, Ashley, and our son, Jack."

"Hi, guys!" a specialist named Audrey Magoun said. Audrey shook Jack's hand, and even through his gloves he could feel her strong grip. "Your friend

Nicky here's already been telling us he's not used to such frigid temperatures, especially in April. But that's Denali for you."

"Where I come from it's starting to be spring. So what would you say the temperature is out here, anyway?" Nicky asked, clapping his gloves together with a sound like percussion. "Minus one thousand?"

"Nah, we're in a heat wave," Blake Van Horn exclaimed. "The last couple of days registered a comfy 20 degrees Fahrenheit. Of course, this morning was still a bit nippy at zero."

"Zero?" Nicky's eyes crinkled. "Explain to me again why we're freezing to death in the middle of nowhere for a flipping weasel."

"Wolverine," Ashley corrected.

"Actually, Nicky's right. The wolverine is a weasel of sorts—it belongs to the weasel family, Mustelidae," Olivia told them.

Nicky's face lit up. "See, Ashley? I've done my homework. I even read a book."

"First one?" Jack asked under his breath, but no one seemed to hear.

Holding his hand a yardstick's distance apart, Nicky went on, "The book said that even though those wolverines are only this long—three feet—they're so fierce they can jump on a caribou's back and ride it to death. Man, wolverines are tough."

"No, no, no," Audrey protested. "That's pure myth.

It's exactly those kinds of stories that have caused the wolverine harm."

"But I read it—"

"I realize that, but some of the older books are just plain wrong."

They were off into a discussion of the impact of myths on the wolverine. Jack shoved his hands into his parka and stared at the frozen ground, not willing to join in since they all seemed to be talking to Nicky. It was only a few more minutes before he heard a sound, faint and soft, like distant rain. When he looked down the glossy trail, he saw a team of dogs running toward them, their feet churning up the snow in small bites. Thank goodness Chaz had arrived.

Twelve of the most beautiful animals Jack had ever seen glided up to the lean-to. There were two lead dogs, one with a black and tan muzzle and eyes so bright they looked to Jack like blue marbles. The other had a cream face and golden eyes. Behind the leads, attached to a long harness, were ten more dogs buddied up in rows of two, all with tails curling over their backs in furry question marks. The man standing behind the sled was smaller than Jack had expected, with a pointy, mouse-like face and a thin frame.

"Whoa," he said, hopping off the runners and tipping the sled over on its side. Throwing down what looked like a half of a stirrup with metal teeth, the man stepped on the metal and ground it into the snow, as a kind of brake. Once the dogs had come to a stop they began to bark and leap against the harnesses, in a cacophony of whines and yips. Then the man extended his hand to Steven.

"Hi, I'm Chaz Green," he said loudly. "I'm with the Wolverine Rescue Program. And you are Steve…"

"Steven Landon. I believe you spoke with my wife, Olivia."

"Yes, I'm pleased to meet you," Olivia exclaimed. "I'm so grateful you offered to take the kids. Necropsies can be pretty rough."

"What's a necropsy?" Nicky whispered to Ashley.

"An animal autopsy," she whispered back. "Mom's going to cut open the wolverine bodies to see if she can figure out how they died." Then, to Chaz, Ashley asked, "Mr. Green, can I pet them? The dogs, I mean?"

Chaz grinned, but it was a tight smile that showed no teeth. "Sure thing, little girl. Call me Chaz. You must be Ashley, right? And that's your brother, Jack? And…who is this fine young man? Are you Nicky?"

They all nodded.

Chaz extended his hand and gave Ashley's a firm shake. "Well, Ashley, you should know that my dogs love to be rubbed behind their ears, so make sure you give them a good scratch. The lead dog with the blue eyes is named Kenai, and the tan one's name is Sasha. While you kids get acquainted with my dogs, I'll give the particulars of the times and such to your folks. After that, I promise we'll be off on the adventure of a lifetime. Deal?"

"Deal!" Ashley answered, giving a little hop.

While Chaz joined the rangers, Nicky, Jack, and Ashley began to circle the sled. Rubbing the bottom of his nose with his index finger, Nicky walked around the basket, peering into its small canvas interior. "There's not much room in that sled thing," he sniffed. "How are we all gonna fit?"

Jack ignored the question. Instead, he went straight to the lead dogs. Some of the other dogs had dropped to the ground, rolling and grunting and yapping in the snow. The six that remained standing, including the two leads, quivered in anticipation, straining on the gang line. Jack had to agree with what Blake had told him earlier: These dogs were born to run. All they seemed to want to do was to get on the trail once more, as if their energy could barely be contained in their lean bodies. Jack scratched Kenai behind the ears, first with his gloves on and then with a bare hand. His fingers worked their way through the rough coat down to a silky underlayer. Kenai whimpered appreciatively and gave Jack's hand a tiny lick.

"Okay, kids, listen up. Here's the plan," Chaz announced loudly. "While those scientist types are doing their work, we explorer types are going to head south to Wonder Lake. I expect to be back in four hours."

"Four hours. I've got 11:46 a.m.," Steven said. "So

we'll meet you right here at approximately 4:00."

Olivia raised her hand and shadowed her eyes. "Chaz, it looks like there's a storm coming in. Are you sure that's OK?"

"No worries," Chaz assured Olivia "We're heading down south into open terrain. The storm's to the north."

"It should be fine," Blake affirmed. "Everyone will be back before that storm hits. I checked the weather report this morning. We're in the bubble."

Chaz pointed into his sled. "Right under the cushions in the basket is a whole bunch of survival gear. If anything did happen, we'd be sitting pretty. But I tell you what—if any flakes start to fall, we'll come right back. I won't take any chances."

Olivia looked to Steven, who gave a quick nod.

Righting his sled, Chaz motioned for Nicky to get into the sled basket and sit closest to him. "Ashley, you take the middle. Jack, you be in front." When Jack began to protest, Chaz told him he thought it was best for balance to have him in front.

"But Ashley won't be able to see around me!" Jack argued. "She should be in front!"

His father shot him a look and said firmly, "Son, Chaz knows what he's doing. Sit where he tells you."

Jack sighed. How could he explain that he didn't want his sister leaning against Nicky? Lips pursed, he watched as Nicky got in first, then Ashley. Finally Jack wedged himself between his sister's legs. It was cramped inside the basket, but not too bad, except for when Nicky's big boots drilled into his sides.

"Hey, Jack, you've got a perfect view of the wrong end of a dog," Nicky laughed.

"Reminds me of your face," Jack replied.

Chaz placed his feet on the runners, releasing the claw brake.

"Wait!" Olivia cried. "Before you go, I have one other question that has puzzled me. I was wondering if you had an opinion on it, Chaz."

"What's that?" he asked, raising his eyebrows.

"It's just that a wolverine's range is pretty huge, and they're fierce when it comes to defending their own territory. I just can't understand how two males were found so close together without a mark on either one. You found them about 20 feet apart, right? You didn't move those bodies at all?"

Chaz looked startled. "Absolutely not—I didn't touch 'em. That's exactly how I found them, Dr. Landon, and that's a fact."

"Do you have any thoughts on how two *males* were that close?"

Shrugging, Chaz said, "I'm not a scientist, so I have no idea about the male part. They all look the same to me."

A look clouded Olivia's face. She seemed to be turning something over in her mind.

"I wish I could be of more help," Chaz rushed on.

"Thing is, the last year of my life has been dedicated to the wolverines. No offense to grizzlies and the like, but the grizz and the wolf have more people protecting them than you can shake a stick at. Not the wolverines. I don't know, maybe it's their feistiness that made me fall in love with them. So to find two of them dead...." He paused, then awkwardly cleared his throat. "Dr. Landon, you can count on me to help in any way I can," he finished quickly. "I just wish I could help you more. It's really a mystery."

"I appreciate that," Olivia said, nodding. "Well, have fun mushing, kids."

"We will," Ashley answered excitedly.

"That's the ticket. Ready?" Chaz cried. "Let's *go!*"

Feeling a quick tug on the line, the dogs leaned into their harnesses and, with a burst of energy, exploded onto the snow-covered tundra.

CHAPTER FIVE

Chaz yelled out, "Gee," and the sled turned seamlessly to the right. Jack could feel the arctic wind in his face; it turned his cheeks numb with cold. Blake had been right, this was like flying. Beside him trees whizzed by in quick succession, some of them at fantastic angles. Beyond the trees, in the distance, Jack saw mountains sculpted by ice and water and wind. The tops of the mountains themselves were barren and silent looking under their shroud of white. Jagged peaks rolled one into another, as if multiplied by mirrors.

"See those trees growing all crazy-like?" Chaz asked, pointing to a stand of black spruce. "Around here, that's what we call a drunken forest. Seems like they're just gonna topple over."

"I think they look like the trees out of a Dr. Seuss book," Ashley said. "Look at how they bend toward the ground, with those big bush things on the top. Those trees are weird."

"That they are. And you never know what's hidden in there, just watching you glide by. Guess what I saw when I was out mushing two weeks ago," Chaz rattled on, not waiting for an answer. "I saw me a grizz. Yes I did. I was mushing the Lower Savage, only then it was just me and five dogs when out from the trees comes this big old bear. Kenai and Sasha got real nervous, but I just gave them the command. I said, 'On by!' To a sled dog, that means don't-you-go-and-get-distracted-by-anything-you-just-keep-right-on-a-going. And that's exactly what they did. That bear was no more than 30 feet away."

"So did it run after you?" Nicky asked.

"Nah. I was lucky, though, 'cause grizz'll go for a dog team. My heart was a-pumpin' like crazy, but we made it. I thought to myself, 'Chaz, you just dodged a bullet. *This must not be your day to die.*'"

"Wow," Jack said, trying to imagine it. "Mom told me that wolverines are called little bears. Have you ever seen a live one? A wolverine, I mean."

"Heck no. I've seen their tracks, though. And I've definitely seen the damage they cause. But it's a rare thing to spot one roaming in the wild. I haven't been that lucky. And to find two dead ones—well, that sure was strange."

"Why'd you start the Wolverine Rescue Program?"

Chaz shrugged his small frame. "Like I said to your folks, I like how fierce they are and how they make their own way. Plus, that wolverine—he don't take nothin' from no one. Some even say they're mystical. Way back a friend of mine got tired of a wolverine that kept slashing up his food cache—swore he'd take care of it. I warned him it was bad luck to kill 'em 'cause natives say they're magic. But my friend, he did it anyway. Yep, he shot that wolverine dead."

"That's stupid. If it was me, I could have rigged my cache to keep the wolverine out," Nicky bragged.

"So, you know what happened to my friend who shot the wolverine?"

"What?" all of them asked.

"Later that same day, my friend's Jeep rolled over, and he was killed." Chaz waited a beat before saying, "My point is it pays to respect the ancient ones. I put that story on my Web site. Lots of donations rolled in because of it. Folks really liked the magic angle."

Nicky scoffed, "I don't believe in magic. You said you dodged a bullet, and your friend didn't. Must have been his day to die."

Chaz's voice became flinty. "Must have been. You just never know, do ya?"

They fell silent. The trees disappeared, replaced by vast, open tundra that glittered in the sun like white sand. The dogs seemed to chew up the earth, one glassy mile after the other, as they followed Moose Creek toward Wonder Lake. Ashley asked about the dogs, so Chaz told them that the two dogs directly behind the leads were called swing dogs, then the next three pairs were team dogs, followed up by a pair of wheel dogs. Each did a different job, working in tandem to keep the sled sliding across the snow.

After an hour on the sled, Chaz seemed to run out of things to say, which was fine with Jack. In the silence that followed, other thoughts—the ones Jack had tried to push down—began to nibble at him like termites. First came Nicky and his fantastic story. It didn't make sense, not any of it. Why all the lies about his dad being a spy? What was Nicky doing here? And why, Jack wondered, was Ashley so ready to believe him? He wished he could just give himself over to the wind and the snow crystals that stung at his skin and get lost in all the open beauty unrolling before him like a silken scroll. Instead he kept returning to what Nicky had announced under the flash of the aurora borealis. "You don't know how crazy I can be," he'd told them. Well, Jack thought he knew.

Nicky was a crazy punk, and the worst part was that Ashley couldn't see it. Unbidden, Jack's mind flashed to the picture of Nicky with his arm around Ashley. Shaking his head he tried to get the image out of his mind, but he couldn't jar it free. She said she liked him. His own sister had been fooled by Nicky's wild story—how dumb was that? Maybe she didn't think it mattered if you let someone spin a CIA fantasy, but it mattered to Jack. And, he had to admit, it wasn't just that he cared about truth. The real reason ran deeper.

It was the fact that his sister had chosen to trust this strange kid over him—that was at the core of it. Even though Jack had sounded a clear warning, his sister still believed the punk. Nibble, nibble, nibble; the irritation kept biting him. His cheeks were frozen from the spray of snow the dogs kicked up as they ran. Jack wished they could go back to Kantishna. A necropsy couldn't be that bad. Besides, no one said they had to watch!

Suddenly, Ashley cried, "Up ahead—that huge mountain—is that Denali?"

"It is," Chaz answered.

"Oh my gosh, it's amazing!"

There, to the south, rising like an enormous crown, was a massive mountain with a peak that seemed to scrape the very bottom of the sky. Jack had been born and raised in Jackson Hole where the Tetons had always dazzled him, but this—this was almost too much to take in. The sky was a clear turquoise that framed the mountain like a jeweler's velvet. At the base of the mountain, a long stretch of clouds hovered over the foothills in an endless streamer, bisecting the view. Just beyond, emerging from the snow, was the jewel of Denali, its scalloped ridges tinted in shades of palest blue and silver-white as if light itself had carved the facets. It was immense, brilliant, incomprehensible.

Jack breathed it in, instantly glad he'd been here to see it, Nicky or no Nicky.

"Denali is 20,320 feet high—the highest mountain on the North American continent," Chaz told them. "It is also called Mount McKinley. In fact, that's its official name, but everyone around here calls it Denali. Sometimes, if you get here on a clear day, you can see the mountain reflected in Wonder Lake."

"Just look at it," Ashley said, her voice reverent, while Nicky added, "That is one big mountain."

Ashley turned to Chaz. Her stocking cap had been pulled almost to the bridge of her nose, but a few tendrils of hair had escaped. The wind blew them over her cap like dark, curling shoots. "You know so much about Denali—have you lived in Alaska all your life?"

"Nooo. I'm originally from the lower 48. About five, no, six years ago, I decided it was time to get away from all the city life, so I came up here. See, I thought the city was wild, but I had no idea what Alaska could dish out. Almost died my first winter. Now I got snowshoes and a shovel and candles and all kinds of stuff packed in my sled, 'cause the backcountry will kill you if you're not prepared. Even carry a gun, just in case I tangle with an animal that won't let me go my way. One thing I know, this place is wilder than the city."

Ashley asked, "Where were you from?"

"I was born in Texas, but the years before Alaska I spent in Pennsylvania. Philadelphia, to be exact."

Jack felt, rather than saw, Nicky stiffen as he asked, "You lived in Philly?"

"Yeah. You're from Philly, too, aren't you?" Chaz answered coolly. His voice had become as frosted as the air. "It's amazing, huh? The world seems to be such a big place, but in the end, everybody knows everybody, right? So how'd you get from there all the way to Jackson Hole, Nicky? Did your daddy take you there?"

Jack turned to see Nicky stammer, "I…I don't know."

"Why's that? You seem to be a pretty big kid to not know how you ended up somewhere."

Chaz's jaw tightened as he gazed straight ahead. He had small eyes that were set deep, so deep they were hard to read, and the expression on his face was as blank as a sheet of white paper, but those eyes—they kept zeroing in on Nicky. A smile curled the edges of his lips as he asked, "So where's your dad now?"

"He's…gone."

"Gone? Doesn't sound like much of a dad to just up and leave you."

"My dad is none of your business!" Nicky flared.

"Nicky!" Ashley scolded, "don't be rude!"

"Stay out of this, Ashley," Nicky snapped. "You don't have—just stay out of it!"

Leaning over the handle bow of the sled, Chaz said, "You remind me of my wolverines, kid. Fierce. Maybe a bit nasty, even. But I can deal with that. Oh, yeah, I can deal." His gloved hand moved smoothly over his chin, like a snake. The dogs kept running, faster now, making Jack's eyes teary from the wind.

"Um, Chaz," Ashley began, trying to change the subject, "do you know any other stories you could tell us about the wolverines?"

Chaz shook his head. "I'm fresh out of stories, kid. Why don't you ask Nicky here to tell some stories. I bet he knows a lot of them. I even bet his daddy's the kind that likes to talk, although in my experience, people who talk are sorry in the end. Am I right, Nicky?"

Nicky didn't answer. There was something very wrong here, Jack sensed. It was as if currents were running beneath the water, forces that pushed in unseen ways that were cold and deep and unfathomable. Chaz seemed to be enjoying a truth that only he and Nicky understood, and Nicky looked scared. Then Chaz yelled at his dogs, and they began to run faster still.

Ashley looked at Jack and mouthed *What's going on?* but he could only shrug in reply before he turned to face forward again. Even if they wanted to end this bizarre episode there was nothing they could do, not out here in this wilderness. They kept mushing along the frozen river that wound through the woods like a piece of discarded string, then onto a road, and back to the creek bed. Once again the trees thickened, a shoulder-to-shoulder army of fir trees and spruce. The riverbed forked into two main branches, one to the left, and one to the right.

"Haw!" Chaz cried. At the fork the dogs veered off to the left, and from the shadows Jack could tell they were curving to the east. They rode on, slipping past small clots of wood and hills where the snow had sheered off rock faces, past more sweeping meadows polished smooth by the wind. Clouds in the north were darkening the sky to an ominous steely gray, although Chaz seemed unconcerned as they raced on. Jack tried to convince himself that everything was going to be all right. But something deep in his gut was twisting.

"Chaz," Ashley cried, "we're getting farther from the mountain."

"Seems that way," he agreed.

"Maybe we should go back."

"We can't go back now—our fun is just starting! It's only us and the wild, wild animals. Hey, Nicky, why don't you keep an eye out for a wolverine? I heard that some guy caught one right at the base of that mountain in a trap."

Jack corkscrewed all the way around so that he was facing Chaz, and Ashley did the same. Chaz smiled, exposing all of his teeth. "Actually, I think I'll just go ahead and tell you the truth. See, that's the problem with crime—you can't tell anyone when you've done something truly unique." He pumped his thumb into his chest. "I'm an original. I caught those wolverines and turned tragedy into cash." Raising his hands as if he were a criminal surrendering, he declared, "I might as well confess all the way. It was me. I dumped the wolverines."

"What—what are you talking about?" Jack gasped.

"I got me one wolverine here, and then I caught me four more way out in the wilderness. Kept them in cages until I was ready. Nasty suckers—meaner than spit. No one will ever figure out how I did 'em in. See, I figured they might take a blood sample and check for disease or maybe poison, but I'm smarter than that. There's no poison. So five wolverines, all dead from unknown causes, found in the snow near Kantishna— the publicity was worth its weight in gold. It was ex- actly what my Wolverine Rescue scam needed."

Was Chaz playing some kind of sick joke? Nicky stared straight ahead, his face stone.

Squinting, Chaz seemed to look off into the distance. "Didn't think about them being all males, though," he added, making a clucking sound. "Your mom caught that mistake. She's pretty sharp. Well, I guarantee she won't figure out the rest. Anyway, I put pictures of those pathetic wolverines right on my Web site. Along with a bleeding-heart story, those photos really tugged on the emotions. Credit card donations poured in."

Ashley's voice filled with horror. "Chaz?…"

But Chaz kept talking as if he were telling them a story about the weather. "Do you know how much money I already got from suckers who thought the wolverines were in trouble? Two hundred and twenty thousand dollars. Two-hundred and twenty thousand, and my plan had just barely begun. That would have been big for sure, but it's all over now, thanks to Nicky here. They called me, Nicky, right from Philly. Gave me another job to do." Reaching over, he ruffled the top of Nicky's head. Nicky jerked away.

"You're my job now, kid."

Jack's heart jumped. "Are you serious?" he cried. If Chaz was joking, his mind must really be twisted.

"So I had to clean out my bank account. When I'm done with you kids, I'll be headin' on down to Mexico. It's a pity, though. I really think my dead wolverine thing would have scored big." Chaz suddenly burst out laughing. "What are you lookin' at, Jack? You look like your eyes are gonna pop right out of your head. Hey, I'm just messing with you. I wouldn't think of trapping an animal—I'm the originator of the Wolverine Rescue Program, remember?"

"I...I don't understand," Ashley stammered. Her hands gripped the sides of the sled like claws.

Jack didn't either. This man was either a real wacko, totally out of his mind, or else he was telling the truth and the three of them were in serious danger. He could no longer even see Denali's tip, which meant they had been heading in the wrong direction. They were going south now, close to a different mountain with a high face, the bald kind with no trees to mar its pristine whiteness. Chaz suddenly called out a firm, "Whoa!" When the dogs danced to a stop, he jumped on the brake and threw out a hook line. The dogs barked in protest, straining at their harnesses.

"I said 'whoa!'" Chaz cried again. This time the team settled into a controlled agitation. Jack looked around wildly. They could run, but there was nowhere to run to. Only snow and the empty mountains.

"Now, here's the thing, kiddies," Chaz said, turning on them with cold eyes. "I thought it would really be fun to take a little plane ride. Me and my dogs and you, Nicky. Hate to play favorites, but I can only take one. My airplane's parked just a little farther on, right past that ridge there."

"I'm not going anywhere with you," Nicky answered quietly. A strange expression had etched across his face—half fear, half resignation.

"Take us back to Kantishna!" Jack demanded, wondering again if Chaz was playing some kind of sick joke. But Chaz ignored him. All his attention seemed focused on Nicky. Biting the finger of his right glove, he pulled it off, then found the tab of his parka and yanked it down, calmly placing the glove in his pocket. "Oh, you'll want to go on this ride with me, Nicky. Tell your friends to get out of the basket so we can take care of business. You know what this is about."

The words seemed to hover in the cold air, and for a moment Jack didn't connect them until suddenly he understood. Chaz was kidnapping Nicky. He intended to take Nicky and leave Jack and Ashley in the frozen wilderness.

"Jack—Ashley—get out." Chaz demanded harshly, not bothering to disguise the threat. "This isn't your business. It's between me and Nicky."

"No!" Jack exploded. His heart was beating so wildly he thought his chest might blow apart. "We're staying right here in the sled—all of us. You've got to take us back to Kantishna. This is crazy, Chaz. You're not funny. Take us back!"

Like a dog showing its teeth, Chaz pulled back his lips threateningly. "Get that sister of yours and run along. Nicky has already cost me plenty."

"Do what he says," Nicky told them stiffly.

"But we'll freeze to death out here!"

Chaz gave a short bark of laughter. "That's what I'm counting on." He slipped his hand into his parka and pulled out a silver, snub-nosed gun. Although Jack's brain felt thickened by images and words that didn't make sense, this he understood: Gun. Chaz had a gun, and it was pointed right at the base of Nicky's skull.

Ashley's hands flew to her mouth. "Chaz, no!"

Chaz looked down at Ashley, but his eyes held no emotion at all. He bit off every word as he said, "I'm going to tell you and your brother one more time. Get out of my sled."

Jack sat frozen. What should he do? What could he do? All he could see was the gun.

Now Chaz spoke only to Nicky. "My boss says your daddy will cooperate once he hears your voice on the phone. You're the one I want. Tell them."

"Ashley," Nicky said hoarsely. "Get out of here."

Neither one of them moved. Jack felt as if his brain had disconnected from his body.

"Are you two deaf?" Chaz demanded, waving his gun in the air. "Leave or I will shoot your friend right in the head." His face contorted. *"Now!"* he screamed, so loud his voice echoed off the northern face of the mountain, the *now, now, now,* bouncing into the air until it disappeared like a dying note. Then shoving the muzzle in Nicky's neck, he cocked the gun.

Jack and Ashley scrambled out of the basket and stood woodenly in the snow. The color had drained from Nicky's face. "It's OK, Ashley," he whispered. "Try to save yourself."

"How noble!" Chaz pulled back the gun, leaned down, and with a quick jerk pulled up the snow hook and dropped it beside his feet. Resting the gun on the handle of the sled, he said, "You'll talk to your dad, and after that, who knows? It could be like what happened to my friend—remember that little story I told, Nicky? Well, guess what? This just might be *your* day to die."

CHAPTER SIX

A wind gusted up and scoured the riverbed, spinning a gauzy curtain of powdered snow that hit Jack full in the face. The coldness stung him, waking his senses, jump-starting his fear-frozen mind. He had to think, and he had to do it fast. The dogs barked furiously.

Ashley took a small step toward the sled.

"Stay where you are!" Chaz ordered. His arm spun around to aim the gun right at Ashley's chest. His eyes were deadly.

Jack could hear the quaver in his sister's voice as she asked, "Why are you doing this?"

Chaz just snickered. The gun dropped to his hip as he grabbed the snow hook.

"Don't leave us!" Ashley pleaded.

"It will look like a tragic accident. You two found frozen in the Denali wilderness, while Nicky's remains—

lost. They'll figure the wild animals got him. And me? Oh, they'll never find me. I'll be long gone. I've got my plane parked at the Glen Creek airstrip. I'll put my basket and dogs and Nicky right inside, and then we'll be off. Me and Nicky are about to disappear."

"But why?" Ashley demanded. "I don't understand!"

Chaz didn't answer. Instead, he snapped the hook beneath the runner. His right hand still clutched the gun, which once again hovered dangerously close to the back of Nicky's head. The sled pitched forward, but Chaz's fierce command of "whoa" once again held the dogs in check.

What could Jack do? Different scenarios flashed through his mind, considered for an instant and then discarded. He and Ashley could turn and try to run, but Chaz could pick them off like tin ducks in an arcade. They could stay where they stood, statues in the snow, yet standing still would make them perfect targets if Chaz decided to shoot. And what about Nicky?

He watched Nicky's hands grip the sled, saw his eyes widen with fear, his lips part slightly as he took several quick gulps of air. If Jack rushed the basket, it might give Nicky the chance to run, but for Jack it would be suicide. All of these thoughts fired through the neurons in his brain in rapid succession. No, there was no answer. They were trapped.

Sasha and Kenai quivered in their harnesses, anxious to go forward and yet compelled by Chaz to stay.

"Whoa," he commanded again as he stepped off the claw break. Jack knew that in a matter of seconds, Chaz, and Nicky, would be gone.

The yapping of the dogs echoed off of the sheer mountain wall. The dogs! They might be the answer. If Jack could spook the dogs—in his mind's eye he saw the sled heave forward, saw Chaz rock back and lose his balance to fall onto the frozen creek bed. If Jack could make that happen, in that split second they'd have a chance to escape. It could work. But how could he spook those dogs? His eyes snapped to the ground where he saw several broken branches with bleached-out needles, and next to them a crooked stick the size of a ruler. None of those could work. If he threw any one of them it would wobble weakly through the air. Out of the corner of his eye he saw a clutch of baseball-size rocks, each with a cap of glittering snow, nestled only inches from his right foot. A rock. Pitched right at the flank of the wheel dog, the rock could send them into chaos. But Jack wasn't sure of his aim. If he missed.…A shudder passed through him as he pictured the barrel of the nickel-plated gun. He couldn't miss. He would get one try, one gamble. There would be no second chances.

Chaz straddled the runners and gripped the handle bow with his left hand. In that split second Jack dipped his knees to grab the closest rock, jerking it hard to pull it out of the snow. His heart began beating so wildly he was afraid his ribs would shatter. At that moment Chaz turned and saw the rock in his hand. Instantly Jack took aim and with every fiber of strength in his body he heaved the rock, hitting the swing dog squarely in its flank. The dog's high-pitched squeal let him know he'd scored the mark.

"Run!" Jack screamed, to Ashley, to Nicky, to himself. *"Run! Run! Run!"*

It seemed as though everything happened at once; the wheel dog shot into the haunches of the team dog in front of him, and then the neck line, tug line, and gang line tangled as the sled surged ahead. Chaz's hand flew up as he lost his balance; a shot split the sky before the gun sailed end over end like the blades of a pinwheel, and then disappeared into a thicket of shrubs. Cursing, Chaz grabbed the handle bow to steady himself at the precise moment Nicky catapulted out of the basket and onto the ground, racing toward Jack and Ashley.

"Whoa!" Chaz stomped on the claw break and screamed again, *"Whoa!"*

"Hurry!" Jack screamed. He grabbed Ashley's hand and almost pulled her off her feet.

A few fist-size balls of snow skittered down the sheer mountain face like beads from a broken string, rolling across the creek bed before disappearing into the other bank. As the dogs barked wildly in a cacophony of sound, Jack realized Chaz barely had control of them.

If he left the team to search for the gun, the dogs would streak away. He was caught in his own web. When Jack glanced back, Chaz was looking at him with such cold hate that Jack felt his blood turn to ice. He knew without a doubt that if Chaz had had the gun, he would have shot Jack right then and there.

Nicky sprinted toward them so fast his feet churned up divots of snow, and then he stopped in his tracks, pivoting to face Chaz. He was panting hard. "Get out of here!" he screamed. Slicing the air with his arm, he cried, "It's over. You can't take all three of us. *Leave us alone!*"

"You think you've won?" Chaz answered vehemently, still trying to steady himself on the sled. The sound from the dogs bounced up the face of the mountain, causing more snow to skitter down. Jack looked above him, at the smooth snow that glimmered like a sheet of glass. A memory from scouting jarred him. Sound. Snow. Gunshot. Snow.

"I've got the dogs!" Chaz raged. "In a few hours it will be 20 below and your blood will freeze solid. You may have dodged a bullet, but Denali will do the rest."

As if to affirm his words, a gust of wind danced around them, blowing yet another curtain of crystals through the wild emptiness.

"Get out of here!" Nicky screamed.

"You'll never make it."

"I'll make it!" Nicky cried defiantly. "You tell them

Nicky Milano won. You'll never find us again—not me, not my dad!"

Chaz let go of a stream of curse words, then released the claw break. Leaning forward, he shouted the command "Hike! Let's go!" The dogs jerked forward, slowed because of their tangled lines. Once again a funnel of snow swirled around them like the spirit of a whirlwind, licking at the back of Chaz's sled as he took off toward the east.

Just then Jack heard a crack like a tree splitting from frost, only a hundred times louder. It was coming from behind him, not in the direction of the retreating dog sled. His eyes flew to the mountain's peak.

More balls of snow skittered down like balls of yarn. Snow. Sound. Dogs barking. The crack of the gun. Each thought raced through his mind, faster than the tick of a watch. He knew. Instantly he grabbed Ashley's arm and pulled her toward the direction they'd come, but before he'd taken two steps, he knew he was too late. There was another crack and a rumble, as if thunder had broken through the clouds. But this was a deeper sound, louder and more frightening than any storm.

The first things he saw were the branches. Tips of spruce swayed in the arctic wind, but a flick of motion above the tree line drew his gaze past the smattering of trees, up to where the sheer mountain face touched the sky. An enormous plate of snow broke free, as if a giant knife had sliced off a piece of cake.

There was no time to move, no place to go even if he could. A tidal wave of snow, ten feet deep and as wide as the mountain, had come loose, roaring down the mountainside like a tsunami of crushed ice. The trees that stood in its path were broken like so many toothpicks. In that brief second, Jack called out the only word that came to mind.

"Swim!" That was the last thing he said before the wall of snow hit him full force.

White. His world was suddenly pure white as his body got dragged down into a colorless ocean of snow. He tumbled in a cartwheel, righted himself, then felt himself clamped in a vise more powerful than he could comprehend. A tree snapped in half as it hit a rock, like a bone fractured clean through. He, and it, were help-less against the force of the avalanche. Nothing but white. Nothing but cold.

Snow filled his mouth, and for a terrifying moment he couldn't breath. *Swim!* The command came from somewhere deep inside. He had to keep his head up, or he would be buried forever in this grave. With his arms pumping, he struggled to ride the wave, always pushing toward the air, praying the rush of snow would stop and then, in what seemed forever but was only a few seconds, it was over. As he slowed to a stop Jack placed his hands over his face to create an air space. Still tumbling end over end, he finally quit moving.

Panic gripped him, and he fought to push it down.

He couldn't let himself give in to the fear, couldn't use up the last second of oxygen in frantic digging that could send him deeper into the snow, couldn't allow himself to feel his own terror. He tried to move his hands— one was encased in snow over his head, the other, his right, still covered his face. He pushed it away from his eyes, moving it a few inches. This was crazy. There was no way to know which direction was up.

"Help," he whispered. The sound was muffled in his own ears. Opening his lids, he saw nothing but gray-white, felt nothing but deep cold. Which way was up? What had happened to Ashley? Think! He commanded himself. Remember.

At a winter camp out for Eagle Scouts, he'd learned about how to survive an avalanche. Spit! That was it. In order to know which way was up, a person caught in an avalanche needed to spit and follow gravity. Pushing as much snow from his face as he could, Jack sucked against his tongue. When he let the saliva go, it dropped from his lips straight into the snow. OK, he told himself. Gravity says the earth is straight down. He pictured it in his mind, and realized that he was stretched out horizontally, as if he were flying over the earth like Superman. The air was above him. If he'd gone the way his instincts had told him, he would have tunneled himself straight ahead and smothered.

With all his strength, Jack pushed his right hand as far above him as he could reach. Clawing with his left, he tried to kick his feet. Up. He had to get up. Once again, he drove his hand up as far as he could, wrenching his body toward the sky. The wall of snow could have buried him ten feet under. If it had, he would die here. No! Keep pushing! He'd already propelled past his air pocket and snow was filling his mouth, blinding his eyes. He made another air pocket, stopped, caught his breath. Fear seized him. He could die here. No, he told himself. The biggest part of survival is mental. Don't panic—stay focused. Push, kick, move. Finally, after what seemed like an eternity, he felt his fingers break free, and then he felt a hard yank that practically pulled his arm out of its socket. He sucked in a huge gulp of frozen air.

"Jack!" he heard his sister scream. "Jack! Hold on!"

Snow was clawed away from his head, and then Nicky clamped his hands under Jack's armpits and jerked him free from his tomb. His legs buckled beneath him. Jack rolled onto his back and took three long swallows of air, sweet and knife sharp in his lungs. He felt Ashley's fingers on his face brushing the snow from his eyes. In the background he heard the dogs barking wildly.

"Ashley—"

"I'm right here. Nicky pulled you free. We're all OK."

"The dogs—"

"We think Chaz got caught in the avalanche," Nicky said. "Serves him right."

"No—I mean the dogs and the loud barking and the gunshot. I should've remembered sooner. Sound triggers an avalanche. I should have made us move. Should have made us. Are you sure you guys are OK?" Jack croaked.

"We're banged up, but man, we made it," Nicky answered, brushing snow from his hair.

"What about you, Jack?" Ashley asked. Her voice quavered.

"I feel like I've been in a rock tumbler." Gingerly, he moved to a sitting position, testing his limbs. Snow had been packed into every crevice, down his neck and into his boots. He was already freezing. "Whoa, my head is scrambled," he moaned. Taking off his glove, he began pulling chunks of snow from his collar.

"I did what you said, Jack. I tried to swim—but—" Ashley's face suddenly contorted, and she began to cry great, heaving sobs. "I—didn't—know where you were and—"

"Don't cry, Ashley," Jack told her. "I'm serious. You'll need the energy."

Every inch of Ashley was covered with white, as though she'd been rolled in dough. Her knit cap was gone, as well as one glove, but she was alive and standing with Nicky's arm around her shoulders like a vise. *That arm again!* Nicky's hair stood from his head in snowy clumps, and his cheek had been scraped raw. Blood seeped out of the scrape and trickled down onto his parka in a thin, red ribbon. *"Shhh,"* he told Ashley in a hushed voice. "We're alive. That's all that matters."

The dogs' barking became more urgent. Jack looked out at the field of white, its former glassy surface now mottled with chunks of snow. Broken branches, rocks, and tree trunks had been flung around like confetti on a sheet. They could have been killed. Easy.

Rolling to his knees, he stood and took a few wobbling steps in the dogs' direction. "We should help the dogs."

"Yeah. At least some of them are alive," Nicky agreed. "They're really howling—I bet they're still tied to the sled."

"What about Chaz?" Jack asked.

"I thought of that. We'll look to see if he's digging up his dogs. If he is, we'll turn and go the other way. If not, we'll help the dogs. They don't deserve this."

Jack shook his head to clear it. "No, that's not what I meant. If Chaz got buried in the avalanche, he's suffocating right now."

Nicky stiffened. "So? I say if he dies, it's justice."

"I know, but…but can we really do that?"

"Watch me," he spat. "I can do it easy."

Ashley bit the edge of her lip. "Was Chaz a bad spy?"

"Yeah. Remember, I told you they were after me. You believed me, but Jack didn't. Right, Jack?" He cocked his head. "You thought I was full of it. What do you think now?"

Jack dropped his gaze. Of course it was true. He'd thought terrible things of Nicky, who had been telling the truth all along. It was hard to remember all those bad feelings, especially when Nicky was the one who'd pulled him from the snow. "I'm sorry I didn't trust you, Nicky," he told him.

With a curt nod, Nicky said, "Apology accepted," and held out his hand for Jack to shake. That effectively removed the arm from Ashley's shoulders, so with a smile, Jack shook hands.

The dogs' howls kept splitting the sky like sirens. "We gotta start digging," Jack said, but when he tried to take a step his legs nearly buckled beneath him. He grabbed Ashley's arm to steady himself.

"Yeah, digging to save the dogs," Nicky said.

"But how can we save the dogs and not the man?"

"That Chaz is a waste of skin!" Nicky fumed. Pointing toward trees that were still standing, he cried, "What if he's out there, watching, waiting for us?"

"And what if he's dying while we're arguing?" Jack shuddered as he remembered his own tomb of snow. "Can you live with that?"

"I can!" Nicky blazed. "Don't be stupid, Jack." Turning toward Ashley, he asked, "You think I'm right, don't you? Don't you?"

"Ashley, Chaz is still a human being," Jack said weakly. "We can tie him up with the dog harness— whatever you think is right. I just can't let a person suffocate in the snow." But it was no use. From the look in Ashley's eyes he could tell she would do whatever Nicky suggested. The alliance had shifted. Jack would have to go it alone.

Turning on his heel, he headed toward the dogs' crescendo of yaps and cries. He knew that in some ways what he was about to do didn't make sense, and there was no doubt Nicky had every right to be vengeful. But at the end of the day, Jack would have to live with himself, so he had to try to save a life, even if it was an evil life. He paused as he tried to calculate the quickest path across the snowfield. Some of the snow was littered with debris, while other parts looked like white carpet.

Suddenly he felt his sister's hand on his elbow and saw that she was walking in tandem with him once again, her boots thumping lightly in the snow. "You can stay if you want, Nicky," she called over her shoulder. "I'm going with Jack."

CHAPTER SEVEN

"Hold up, I'm coming!" Nicky cried. "I don't like it, but I'm coming."

"Good," Ashley said.

Ashley's smile irritated Jack. Hadn't his sister just sided with him? He'd been hoping Nicky would stay away but now, once again, they were three. Well, Jack had bigger problems to worry about than Nicky Milano. The howling of dogs rang through the air; in the distance Jack saw a dark shape that looked like an arm reaching up from a sinking ship. For a split second he thought it belonged to Chaz until he realized it was one of the dogs. Jack began to breathe again.

Sasha howled as if he'd been shot. "Don't worry, we're almost there!" Ashley cried.

"I still say we free the dogs and leave Chaz buried. Guys like him have nine lives," Nicky said grimly. "Like in a horror movie, he'll come back. He's just too mean."

The path of the avalanche, as wide as the length of a football field, ran from the very top of the mountain all the way to the creek bed and beyond. Although smooth slabs of snow had sheared off the mountain wall, the avalanche path was marbled with chunks that ranged in size from pebbles to grapefruit to bowling balls. Here and there Jack saw the scattered remains of trees, their broken limbs resting at crazy angles. An enormous force had been contained in that roaring mass of snow. It was as if a bomb had gone off—nature's bomb that had instantly swept everything in its path.

And yet, now that its fury was gone, the mountain seemed to have settled back to sleep. A mist churned by the avalanche hung in the air, muting colors of trees and sky as if they were covered with tissue paper. Every few seconds a stream of snow would break free from spruce needles, cascading in tiny chutes until the branches once again sprang toward the hidden sun. It would have been beautiful if it hadn't been so deadly. They pushed on, struggling through snow that seemed to grow thicker with each step.

"What time is it?" Jack asked.

Nicky jerked up his coat sleeve to check his watch. "Two thirty-six. I figure we were hit about 18 minutes ago. Which means—"

"We'd better go faster," Ashley finished up. She didn't add what he knew they were all thinking, that if Chaz was under the snow, his time was quickly running out. "So come on!" she cried.

From the sound of the dogs, Jack could tell Chaz had made it to the farthest side of the path of the avalanche. If not for the huskies' cacophony, they would never have known how to find the sled. The yelps served as a beacon, drawing them to the site like a lighthouse drew ships.

"Do you think the dogs' noise'll cause another slide?" Ashley asked nervously.

"No. We're right in the path of the one that already fell. We'll be OK." Jack looked into the remaining trees, and for a moment his heart jumped into his throat. There, perched in the thick foliage of a spruce tree, sat a boreal owl. From the mottled shadows, its large yellow eyes seemed to watch his every step. He must be getting jumpy, maybe because Nicky had mentioned horror movies and the owl looked eerie. Get a grip, he told himself. Odds were that Chaz lay buried with the sled. And yet, Jack and Ashley and Nicky had defied the same odds by escaping the snow's grasp. Maybe Chaz had, too.

The barking became deafening. The two lead dogs, Kenai and Sasha, had clawed a crater in the snow around them—a hole three feet deep and four feet wide. Still attached to the gang line, they frantically strained against their harnesses, but they were caught like flies in the web of neck line and tug line. A few harnesses lay empty on the ground, which meant, to Jack's relief, that some of the dogs must have escaped. When the dogs spotted them coming they became even more frenzied.

"You're safe, we're here now," Ashley cooed to them. She immediately began trying to work them free from the tangles, soothing them with a steady stream of "hush now" and "you'll be free soon." First she went to help Sasha, but another team dog was so panicked that it knocked Ashley flat. Rocking back up, she called out, "Whoa," so loudly that they quieted for a moment before they surged around her again. Clearly, the dogs were terrified.

Nicky dropped to his stomach to peer into the hole the dogs had made, scooping out snow with his gloved hands. "Yo, don't look in here," he called out to Ashley. "Some of the dogs didn't make it. There's at least two of them, maybe three bodies."

"Are you sure they're dead?" Jack asked.

"Yeah," Nicky replied. "I'm lookin' at 'em. I know what dead looks like."

"Any sign of Chaz?"

"Nope."

"Can you unhook the dead dogs from the line?"

"I think so. Give me a minute."

Grunting as he worked, Nicky released some lines that Jack couldn't see. Then, fingering a carabiner clip that attached the main line to the front of the sled, he said, "Move back, guys. I'm going to free the line."

"No—wait—" Jack cried, grabbing the blue lead, but Nicky had already squeezed the clip. Instantly, the line jerked through Jack's fingers, ripping a hole in the palm of his right glove. Ashley made a lunge for it, but the line wrenched through her hands. There was no way she could hold on. The other survivors broke free from the snow, barking furiously. They seemed to be trying to run in different directions until Kenai forged ahead, pulling the rest of them back into a ragged formation— like the *V* shape geese make when they fly through the sky. With Kenai in the forefront the dogs turned to race along the creek bed and disappeared behind a bend.

"You shouldn't have unclipped the whole line!" Jack told Nicky harshly. "We could have used the dogs to get back to Kantishna. Or at least we could have used them to stay warm. Now they're gone."

"Never mind," Ashley broke in. "Yelling doesn't help anything, not now. If we're going to look for Chaz, then you better dig."

But first they had to pull out the bodies of the three dead dogs, a disheartening job. Only minutes earlier, those beautiful animals had been racing along the tundra, bursting with energy. Now they lay limp on the surface of the snow, with the life that had surged through their agile bodies extinguished forever. The eyes that had glowed with the joy of running now saw nothing; those muscles that had strained to leap ahead had become immobile. Cold. Dead. Finished. How fragile life could become, Jack thought, and how easily it could end. As he turned away from the mournful sight of the dead dogs, he realized what a miracle it had been that he and Ashley and Nicky had survived. It could have turned out differently…but there was no time to think about that. He had to dig.

The brush bow at the end of the sled protruded, just barely, from the pit, like the arc of a boomerang. Bend and dig, thrust away, dig again in snow that seemed to be congealing like concrete. "What time is it now?" Jack asked.

Nicky read the face of his watch. "Two forty-six."

"That means Chaz has been under at least…28 minutes. He can't survive more than an hour down there."

"A storm's coming in. I say we take care of us."

"Yeah, well, we already know what you say, but Ashley and I think different, remember?" Jack's fingers were stiff from digging, and yet they'd barely made a dent in the snow around the basket. What if they uncovered Chaz's dead body? He shuddered at the thought. It had been harsh enough to deal with the three dead dogs. A deceased human would be infinitely worse. Jack had never seen a dead person, not ever, and he didn't much want to start now.

"If we're going to keep digging, we all need to help," Nicky told him. He immediately dropped to his knees and started clawing at the tip of the sled. "Ashley, can you dig with one hand?"

"I could try, but my fingers are freezing!" She shook her bare hand like a rag. The skin on her right hand—the one that had no glove—was so red it looked scalded. Every few seconds she shoved it under her armpit.

"No, forget it—don't dig—just time us. Here, take my watch."

Nicky pulled off his glove and slid his watch from his arm. "Catch," he said, tossing it to Ashley. If things had been different, Jack would have given his sister one of his gloves to wear, but he had to dig. With no shovel or pick, hands were their only tools.

The snow that had felt like regular snow moments before was settling into the texture of cement. In his mind's eye, Jack saw Chaz, gasping for air against a wall of snow and ice. He clawed faster. More of the sled emerged, but no Chaz.

"Time!" Jack barked.

"Two fifty-eight," Ashley cried. She tucked her hand beneath her armpit again, squeezing it to get the blood circulating.

"We've been at this at least ten minutes now, and we haven't even uncovered half the sled," Jack said, scooping a great armful away from the basket. "This isn't working."

Nicky looked smug. "Just like I thought. You wanna give up?"

"No. In Scouts I learned that after half an hour, the

chances of getting out alive are fifty-fifty. After that—" He didn't finish the sentence. Instead, he began digging even harder until his own hands felt like blocks of ice. One of the laminated runners had emerged, like an archer's bow, then another. As more and more of the basket became exposed, Jack noticed a bag lashed down with straps. The bag might have survival stuff in it, and that was good. Still, no Chaz.

Nicky straightened and rolled his shoulders all the way back, planting his hands on his hips. "Do you think he's even close to the sled? So far we've come up with nada. No hat, no glove, no sign of him. Couldn't he be, like, somewhere else around here?"

"I—I don't know." The thought, although obvious, suddenly hit Jack squarely in the face. Of course Chaz didn't have to be on the sled, or even near it. He hadn't been belted to it. The wall of snow that had come crashing down certainly might have separated Chaz from the sled. The truth was, Chaz could be almost anywhere, dead or alive. Jack looked around at the empty field of snow that seemed to stretch for miles. Finding him would be like searching for a minnow in the ocean.

With the clock ticking and no clue as to where Chaz might be, Jack knew he should give up. But that was exactly what Nicky was hoping for, and that fact alone kept him going. Hoisting himself to his knees, then his feet, Jack picked up one of the broken branches from the ground and snapped off the remaining twigs. While

Nicky watched incredulously, Jack pushed the branch into the snow the way he'd seen rescuers shove poles when they searched for avalanche victims on TV. Prodding all around the sled, thrusting hard to get the branch into the thickening snow, he felt nothing. Poke, poke, poke. The stick left behind a pattern of holes.

"Oh come on, that's not going to work," Nicky chided. "It'd take you all day just to hit a tenth of the avalanche field. Another waste of time."

"Do you have a better idea?"

Nicky frowned, but didn't answer.

"Ashley, what time is it now?" Jack asked.

"Three oh seven," she whispered. Her eyes were wide, so wide Jack could see the whites all around them. "He's been buried in the snow 49 minutes. What should we do?"

Shielding his eyes with one hand, Nicky made a full turn, searching the snowfield as Jack had done. "OK, I'm going to call it. If he's buried, he's gone. If he isn't buried, he could be anywhere out there, and poking the snow with a stick is worthless. We did it your way, Jack, but now we have our own problems. Look at the sky."

Jack's eyes snapped up. He hadn't really noticed the dark clouds descending like a sheet, but they were rolling in ominously.

"Face it," Nicky went on, "this whole idea was boneheaded from the start, which I *tried* to tell you! But you can't admit it when you're wrong, can you, Boy Scout? Listen to me, Ashley. I say we should start walking back along the creek bed. We can follow the sled tracks right back to Kantishna."

"That's suicide! We'll never make it there before dark," Jack fired back. "Walking off unprepared is the worst thing we can do. The three of us should pull that duffel bag out of the sled, then make a shelter and stay put. That storm's moving in fast."

"So you admit we wasted good time looking for Chaz. We could have been on our way."

"I'm not wrong about this! And my sister isn't going anywhere with you!"

"Stop it!" Ashley's voice rang across the snow, clear and loud. The fear had melted from her face, and her eyes looked hot. Lifting her chin, she said, "You guys have been at it since we got to Denali, and I'm so tired of it. Stop! Do you hear me? Just stop!" She stood tall, and Jack suddenly realized she wasn't a little kid anymore—she looked like a real person to be reckoned with. "We can't do this. Not now. You have to quit being so *stupid!* OK, Jack?"

"OK, *Jack?*" Once again, he felt the equation between himself and his sister shifting, like snow crumbling off the mountainside. So Ashley was siding with Nicky—again! A feeling Jack couldn't name surged through him—it wasn't jealousy, exactly. No, it was like water slipping though your fingers when you wanted to hold on, to keep life exactly where it had always been. Jack still wasn't ready to share his sister, especially not with Nicky Milano.

Ashley turned. "OK, *Nicky?*"

Nicky looked startled. Jack felt a surge of satisfaction.

"What is wrong with you two?" she went on. "You're at each other when a human being that was alive an hour ago is trapped under a wall of snow. That's the kind of stuff that's important. Life. Death. The rest is stupid. You're both stupid." Turning away from them, she muttered, "Guys can be so dumb."

For a moment neither one of them said a word. Nicky bowed his head, frowning a little, his hands clasped in front of him while Jack shifted uneasily. She was right, and both of them knew it. It was embarrassing to be brought up short by his little sister. Nicky seemed to feel the same way.

"Nicky, do you think—" Jack began. He cleared his throat. "We should get that duffel bag out of the basket. It has supplies in it."

"You're right," Nicky answered slowly. "Only one of us can fit in the hole. I'll do it. Unless—you know—if you want to."

"You go ahead."

"No, I'll do it," Ashley declared. "I'll fit in there better than either of you."

"All right. You go, girl," Nicky replied.

The wind kicked up, ruffling tufts of Nicky's hair.

A truce had been called. This time it was real, because they'd suddenly realized that survival in Denali wasn't a game. They'd need each other just to stay alive.

The three of them turned toward the basket. Ashley dropped inside the hole, unlashed the duffel bag, and yanked it free. It took a minute to unknot the ropes. Then she looked inside. "There's some stuff, but no food. I'm already hungry."

"We can go a long time without eating. But we're going to need a shelter." Jack studied the darkness rolling in from the mountains. They were facing freezing temperatures, no food, and no shelter, and there was not another human for tens of square miles. If the three of them didn't use every bit of ingenuity they had, it would become their grave as well.

CHAPTER EIGHT

Nicky took a turn rummaging through the duffel bag. Throwing out things left and right, he said, "Chaz sure didn't carry that much on his sled. I thought he told your mom he was prepared with food and everything. What a liar. No food, no first-aid supplies—nothing good. We're in trouble, aren't we?"

"Don't get rid of anything," Jack ordered. "You don't know what we might need. Are you sure there isn't anything to eat in there?"

"Just these, and I'm drawing the line at the fat bars," Nicky exclaimed, holding up one as though he were posing it for a camera. "Yo, read the label. Even if we were stranded out here for a week, you wouldn't catch me touching them. They're for dogs."

Silently, Ashley picked up everything Nicky had thrown onto the snow: the fat bars, a tin bucket, a tin cup, candles, dog booties, and a metal box she pried open to reveal matches.

"Wait, here's something," Nicky yelled, pulling a small camp stove out of the depths of the bag. "We can light the stove to keep warm. I mean, we could if we just had some matches. Oh!" Noticing the open box in Ashley's hand, he added, "All right, Ashley! You've got matches. Now we're cookin'!"

Nicky burrowed into the bag once again. "Great. After all the time we've been digging through the snow with our hands—look what was in the duffel." He held up a shovel and waved it like a flag.

It was a short-handled shovel with a square blade only six inches wide, but it would have made things a whole lot easier if they'd found it earlier. Jack's fingers were still stiff from digging. No one asked if they should keep on shoveling to find Chaz—or Chaz's body—and Jack didn't bring it up, either. Nicky was right; they had to focus on their own survival. A storm was moving in, which meant the three of them were in more trouble than either Nicky or Ashley realized. But Jack understood. He knew the perils of hypothermia, which could easily overtake them all. Darkness was approaching, a storm loomed, and as of now they were completely unprepared. A different kind of clock was ticking.

"Jack, I'm getting cold. The wind's really kicking up." Ashley's nylon hood sparkled with frost, and her eyelashes, too, were frosted white. Jack supposed his own eyelashes looked the same, but Nicky's didn't. Even though the temperature had plunged somewhere around zero, the exertion of digging had flushed Nicky's cheeks.

"So how are we supposed to make ourselves a shelter?" he asked. "There's no hammer or nails in that bag. You got a plan?"

"We'll build with the only thing we've got," Jack told him. "Snow. We'll have to make a snow cave, and we need to get started right away. I don't like the looks of that sky."

Raising his eyebrows, which had started to grow a thin skim of frost, Nicky said, "Tell me what to do."

"Yeah," Ashley echoed. "Tell us."

"First we have to find the right place. Even with the shovel it will take us a long time to dig. We need to make a chamber big enough to stay in."

"But what about the rangers?" Ashley objected. "They won't be able to see us in a snow cave, and I know they'll be out looking for us. When we don't come back on time, Mom and Dad'll get the park people to send a plane."

"Think for a minute, Ashley. We're not where we're supposed to be. Chaz said he was taking us to Wonder Lake, remember? That's where they'll send the planes. Who knows where we are right now?"

"So…you think we'll stay here more than one night?"

Jack dodged the question. How could he know that? "Bottom line is we'll freeze out here without shelter.

I mean freeze—to death! Like I said, we're going to have to work together."

"Go for it, Eagle Scout," Nicky said. Jack whipped his head around to see if Nicky was being smart-mouthed, but his face looked serious. "You can be the boss man. Tell me what to do."

He wished he were as sure about all this as he was pretending to be. "First we have to pick a place where the snow's not so hard to dig," he answered. "Avalanche snow hardens to cement. If we get to the lee side of the creek, we ought to be OK." Oh Lord, I hope that's right, he thought. When he'd gone winter camping with his troop, they'd hiked into a perfectly safe snow basin with no avalanche danger at all. "We need a slope with snow at least six feet deep. Let's go." After they hiked to a slope that looked perfect, Jack began to thrust at the snowbank with the shovel.

"Want me to dig?" Nicky asked.

"No, I want you to remove the snow that I shovel out. First I have to tunnel in about two feet straight back, then angle up for another foot. That's just to make the entrance. I'll dig first while you move the snow away."

"What about me?" Ashley asked.

"You move snow. Shove it away from the entrance."

As Jack dug, Nicky started pulling away the snow so energetically that Jack had to warn him, "Take it easy. You don't want to sweat. If you sweat too much your clothes will get damp, then freeze later. You could get hypothermia, and I don't even want to think about that."

"What's hypothermia?"

"It's when your body temperature gets real low. *Too* low! It can kill."

"Yeah? Well, so can that storm. We'd better get moving, Jack. Flakes are already coming down."

With the three of them working, it went faster than Jack had hoped, although Ashley was hampered by the loss of one glove. She scraped snow awkwardly with her left hand, keeping her bare right hand pulled up inside her sleeve.

After Jack had dug two feet straight back, he began to tunnel upward.

"Let me do some digging," Nicky urged.

"OK. Let me get out first," Jack answered, backing out, then letting Nicky crawl into the hole. "See how it's angling up?" he asked, feeling kind of foolish as he talked to Nicky's backside. "After we make the main room of the cave and light the camp stove and candles, the warm air will stay trapped in there and not escape through the entrance. It's like a—like a split-level house where you go up half a flight of stairs to the main floor."

"Real cool," Nicky grunted, his words swallowed by the tunnel of snow he'd crawled into. One after another, he dropped shovelfuls of snow into the entry hole for Jack and Ashley to scoop out. This snow didn't have anywhere near the mortar-like texture of the avalanche, although it wasn't the powdery kind that skiers like, either. It was somewhere in the middle.

Nicky dug like a Roto-Rooter as more flakes fell from the sky, whipping Jack's cheeks with tiny razor-sharp crystals. "Hold it," Jack called to him. "Let me get in there and take a look."

Nicky backed out. The entrance was so narrow that only one of them at a time could fit inside. When Jack crawled in to check their progress, he had to admit he was impressed. In another hour they should be able to finish carving a room about the area of a pup tent, not big enough for them to stand in, but high enough that they could sit comfortably and maybe curl up together to catch a little sleep. Most important, they could stay warm in there. They could survive.

Jack had estimated the time pretty closely. In an hour and 12 minutes, they completed the snow cave, just after the sun had dipped all the way behind the highest mountain peak. The long-lasting twilight had already tinted the snow to pale amber. Snow pelted them now, and Ashley hugged herself, shivering like a rabbit.

"Ashley, you go first," Nicky told her.

"Th-th-thanks," she replied. One by one, the three of them crawled into the cave. The area turned out to be smaller than Jack had hoped. Roughly four feet square and only three and a half feet high, it gave them barely enough room to sit upright, and not quite enough for them to stretch their legs straight out in front of them.

"It's what I call cozy," Nicky commented. "Very cozy. And dark. Where are the candles, Ashley?"

"Right here." She pulled out the items from the duffel bag one by one: the tin cup, the bucket, the camp stove, the fat bars. Then she reached for Nicky's hand in the darkness to give him the candles and matches.

After Nicky lit a candle and stuck it into the snow floor, he picked up the camp stove to examine it. It looked something like a lamp, with a circular plastic base where a metal cylinder of propane fit snugly. At the top sat a burner similar to one on a gas range, with three metal prongs that would hold a pot or pan. "Let's light this sucker," Nicky said.

"Not yet. First I have to poke a ventilation hole through our roof to the outside. Whenever you burn something in a tight space, you need ventilation or you could die from carbon monoxide poisoning."

"Yo, can everything in Alaska kill ya?" Nicky asked.

"Just about." Jack took the tin cup and pushed it against the snow overhead, rotating it to make a circular hole. When he pulled out the cup, snow came with it—he dumped the snow into the bucket, repeating the process until the bucket was nearly full. "Well, it's going to take me a while to break through," he said, "but maybe you can light the camp stove now, Nicky, if you keep the flame real low. Ashley, set the bucket over the flame so the snow will melt, because we need to get water for drinking."

"Why does the woman always have to do the cooking?" Ashley complained, but she was smiling.

The whole process seemed to take forever: Use the tin cup to scrape a hollow in their ceiling, dump the snow into the bucket, heat the bucket on the stove, get about half a cup of water, take turns drinking it, and keep doing the whole thing over and over again. The cave didn't exactly grow warm, but between the small flame of the stove and the body warmth of the three of them huddling together, the temperature rose enough for Jack to unzip his parka and pull off his gloves.

"Finally!" he yelled, as he pushed his fist through the snow roof to touch outside air. Wiggling his fingers at the dark night, he told them, "We have ventilation! And it isn't snowing too hard right now."

"Do I have to keep drinking this melted snow? I don't want to drink any more—I'm sick of it!" Ashley complained.

"Drink! Your brother commands you," Jack told her.

"Then I'll just have to go to the bathroom."

"Stop drinking! Your brother commands you."

"Ha, ha. Are you sure there wasn't any food in the duffel bag?"

Jack shook his head and tried to close his mind off against his own hunger. "Just the disgusting fat bars. Nicky was right. Listen to the first two ingredients: poultry fat and fish meal. No way I'll ever be that hungry."

"Throw them outside," Ashley ordered. "They stink."

"Sure. I'm not gonna eat them." Jack slid across the narrow floor of snow, which by now was getting pretty compacted. Outside, wind moaned through the trees with deep sighs. Although the snowfall had lightened, the wind had picked up. That meant the tracks from Chaz's dogsled would be totally obliterated by morning, and without those tracks to guide them…well, Jack would face that problem in the morning. With his feet, he kicked the fat bars outside, then shoved the duffel bag against the entrance opening, blocking it most of the way. Scooting backward on his behind, he squeezed himself between Ashley and Nicky, trying not to be too obvious, but not wanting Nicky Milano pressed close against his sister.

For several minutes they sat in silence while Ashley made shadows on the snowy wall of their cave, her fingers moving as delicately as if she were playing piano keys. First a dog shadow, then a bunny, and after that a few more shadows that didn't look like any recognizable creatures. Finally she asked, "Nicky, do you believe in ghosts?"

The question seemed to catch him off guard. "I don't know," he said, staring intently at his chapped knuckles. "Yes. No. Maybe." He shook his head. "Why?"

"I know Jack doesn't, but before we got in the snow cave, I was looking up, and I saw this shadow in the very tip of a fir tree. It was at least six feet long, and it wound around the treetop like a black cloth."

"That was an owl," Jack snorted.

Ashley rapped him sharply with her knuckles. "I know what an owl looks like, and it wasn't an owl. Do you—" She licked her lips, then said, "Nicky, do you think Chaz is dead?"

"I know he is. Ashley, I checked, and there were no footprints anywhere. He didn't come out of that slide."

"Do you think his spirit's spying on us?"

"Nah, I bet he's down there where bad guys go, roasting away."

"But I think I saw him. You and Jack were busy with the tunnel—"

Jack couldn't stand it. It wasn't that he didn't believe in the afterlife, but there was no way a ghost would waste its time zooming around treetops. Spirits must have better things to do. "Come on, Chaz is buried under ten feet of snow. He's dead," Jack protested, hoping he was right.

Nicky leaned his head against the wall and closed his eyes. His hair gleamed copper in the soft light. "When I was six, I thought I saw my mom a few times. My dad would take me to the park, and I swear I saw her, swinging high on the swings, the way we used to."

"Really?" Ashley breathed. "What happened to her?"

"I—I don't want to talk about any of my family. I...can't."

Jack saw his sister swallow her disappointment as Nicky balanced his elbows on his knees, his head bowed so that he closed in on himself, almost like a box that folded flat. The silence was uncomfortable, but Jack didn't know what to say. Drawing people out was Ashley's job.

Suddenly, Ashley brightened. "Hey, I know a wolverine legend that I read in a ranger's book. If we get back home—" She swallowed, and Jack guessed she was asking herself if they would ever really escape, alive, from Denali's bitter cold. After a small, wavering breath, she smiled again. "When we get back, Mom'll be so happy that we know the answer to her mystery. We can tell her that Chaz killed the wolverines." Her dark eyes widened as she made a connection. "Oh my gosh, remember what happened to his friend, the one who shot the wolverine? That guy died. Then Chaz killed five wolverines, and now he's dead, too. Maybe that's why the avalanche got him and not us. Maybe the ancient spirits got him."

"Ashley!" Jack moaned.

But Nicky had raised his head. "I'm listening," he said. "Tell your story."

"It comes from an Alaskan Indian named Shem Pete." Then, closing her eyes like a Native storyteller, Ashley began her tale.

CHAPTER NINE

In the fall, before Denali leaves were painted bright colors, a young Athapascan husband and wife came into the mountains to hunt squirrels. The husband desired the soft squirrel fur to conceal the woman's face from the ice-cold Alaskan winters. His wife was so beautiful he wanted to hide her away, even from himself.

The woman's hair was black as a raven's wing and her eyes were nut brown. Her teeth were as white as whalebone. They said that when she smiled, the sun stayed in the heavens longer and shone a little brighter. Because he was a shaman, the husband used his magic to keep all other people away. Thus, the woman lived her life alone and lonely.

One day, when the shaman had gone to the far hills to hunt, a wolverine caught sight of the woman sitting by herself in her camp. Perched by the fire, she combed *her long hair until the flames shone in her locks like bits of gold. In that instant, the wolverine fell madly in love with the woman. Yet, hidden as he was in the shadow of the forest, he could see that she was not happy.*

Although small in stature, the wolverine could kill a bull moose and tow it away to its lair—that was the strength of the creature. So that very day he kidnapped that young woman and took her into his mountains.

When the shaman returned to find his fire empty, he raised his hands to the skies and made it rain over every single mountain. It rained and rained and rained. The wolverine tried to protect the woman from the ceaseless rain. He took her and tucked her under a rock overhang. When she shivered, he moved her beneath a cliff. But the water kept coming, coming, coming, drumming on the woman's black hair until she was so cold she trembled like a leaf. Although the wolverine tried to warm her by covering her with his tail, he knew she was about to freeze to death. There was only one thing left to do.

When daybreak came, he walked a little way away and shook himself. Then, lifting his voice into the pouring rain, he started to sing.

"Oh Big Wolverine, push those clouds away. Oh Big Wolverine, push those clouds away. Push them with your whole body. Push them with your whole body."

Over and over the wolverine sang. Through the dark clouds the Big Wolverine heard the song. Sweeping the clouds from the sky, he made the sun break through. The warmed earth began steaming all over, because the Big Wolverine had bottled up rain in the heavens once more.

"I took you away so you wouldn't be alone," the wolverine told the woman sadly. "Life is meant to be shared. But if you desire to go back to the shaman, tell me, and I will take you there." He said this even though his heart was heavy.

Without a word she smiled at him, because the wolverine had saved her from being alone. They say that day the sun stayed in the heavens even longer, and shined its brightest. So the two of them hid away in the mountains, and to this day, no one knows where they went. It is said they are hiding still.

#

"That's a really great story, Ashley," Nicky said softly. "I like the way you told it."

"Thank you." Ashley looked up at Nicky with a glance that accentuated her long, thick eyelashes. She even blinked a couple of times. Oh crud, Jack thought.

They'd turned the flame low on the camp stove and had set it on the snow floor in the few inches of space between them. Jack found himself staring at the flickering flame; it was almost hypnotic. Maybe the other two were staring at it too, because for a while no one said anything. Except for their soft breathing, the cave was silent until Jack mused, "Chaz. I wonder if that's a nickname for Charles?"

Nicky answered, "Chaz, Chuck, Charlie—they're all nicknames for Charles. What about it?"

"Nothing. I was just thinking about what you said earlier, when you were playing that game with us. You said 'Charlie is alive.' But…" He stared down at his chapped knuckles. "Chaz is dead."

"Yeah," Nicky agreed. "Chaz was buried alive, and now he's dead."

More minutes passed. Jack could have looked at his watch to see how many minutes, but it seemed like too much of a bother. He just sat still in the silence.

The deathly silence—those words drifted into his brain. Deathly, frozen silence, until…"What's that noise?" he suddenly demanded.

"What noise?" Nicky and Ashley asked.

"Can't you hear it? It's like a…I don't know, but it's coming from outside!"

Nicky straightened. "Quit trying to scare Ashley."

"I'm not!" Jack insisted. "Just listen."

It came again, a crunching sound as if bone were being crushed. Jack could tell Nicky heard it this time, because his mouth set in a thin line.

Ashley scooted closer to Nicky. "It might be the ghost I saw in the trees."

"Come on, that was no ghost," Jack argued. "Look, we're all hearing it now, whatever it is."

"If it's not a ghost, then maybe…." Ashley's eyes widened, "What if Chaz isn't dead?" Her voice rising to a squeak, she looked toward the entrance of the cave and cried, "What if he's coming back for us?"

"I already told you, Chaz was killed in that slide," Nicky said emphatically. "That sounds more like an animal gnawing. *Shhhh*. Just listen."

As they waited in almost complete silence, at first Jack couldn't hear anything except for their own shallow breathing. Then he heard the crunching, and after that a noise that was almost like an object being dragged. Moments passed, and the noise seemed to be getting closer. Was it footsteps Jack heard behind the flimsy duffel-bag door? His heart pounded so loudly, he wasn't sure what was outside and what was hammering in his chest. "I can't stand it—I'm going to take a look," he said. Hoping they wouldn't notice his fingers trembling in the half-light, Jack picked up the candle.

"I'll go with you," Nicky told him.

"No, you stay with Ashley. She's already freaked."

Scooting toward the entrance, Jack heard paper rustling outside. Paper—out here? Then he remembered the fat bars had been wrapped in paper. Some wild creature had come after the fat bars Jack had tossed right outside the entrance. Stupid, stupid, stupid to toss out food like that. Now the question was, what creature had found it?

Then he saw a twitching black nose poking around the edge of the duffel bag, snuffling across the frozen ground. Grizzly? No, too small. The muzzle burrowed in farther—covered with blood! Blood that left streaks on the snow cave's packed entrance. The creature was coming in! Well, not if he had anything to do with it.

Taking a breath, Jack slammed his foot against the animal's snout. It gave out a warning cry, but instead of backing off, it barreled the rest of its body through the makeshift door. Jack gasped! He knew what it was—he'd seen the pictures. *Gulo gulo,* the glutton. He'd just come face to face with the elusive wolverine!

"Did you see that?" he asked, keeping his voice low.

"Yes. Make him go away!" Ashley wailed.

"I'm trying! Those jaws are powerful. I don't want to lose a foot. Oh, man, it's coming back in!"

The wolverine had stopped partway into the cave's entrance to glare fearlessly at them. Its long neck extended, its muzzle slimed with blood, its small eyes glowing as they reflected the candle flame, it looked truly ferocious. A low, guttural growl escaped from its snarling mouth.

"Get out of here!" Nicky cried, grabbing the shovel and beating the snow. "Go!"

"Nicky, don't hurt it," Ashley cried. "It doesn't know."

"I'm just trying to scare the thing. Man, look at those teeth!" When Nicky smacked the snow again hard, the motion seemed to startle the animal. After three or four more warning blows the wolverine backed away until it finally disappeared for good.

Nicky settled back into the cave and grinned. A flush

crept up his cheeks, and he was panting. "What's up with that? Was the wolverine listening to your story and figured he'd take a bow?"

Ashley rolled her eyes. "I don't think so. But that is so strange. I mean I *just* told that story and then one shows up. How weird is that?"

"Not as weird as you think," Jack told them. "He came after the fat bars."

"Maybe, but that doesn't explain what he's chewing on out there. Can't you hear that crunching? I swear that's gotta be bone. Animal bone." Nicky said. "Didn't your mom say wolverines are scavengers?"

"Yeah, they patrol fresh avalanche tracks looking for animals killed by the slide," Jack answered.

"But what is he scavenging?" Ashley asked. "We didn't see anything out there except a lot of snow and a bunch of broken-off branches and—" Her eyes widened with horror. "Oh my gosh the dogs! *He's eating the dead dogs.* I know that's what he's doing—that is so sick and disgusting."

Of course Ashley had to be right. Jack could feel it. He wavered between being grossed out and forgiving the wolverine, because he understood the interactions that bound all life together. Animals in the wild had to survive. Nothing was wasted. Ever.

Ashley squeezed her eyes tight. "I can still hear the sounds—it's too awful. I hate being here—Mom and Dad are probably—" Her voice cracked as she dropped her face into her hands. "Why is this even happening to us? We're stuck here. We might die here, and I don't understand why!"

Out of nowhere, Nicky said, "It's all my fault. I'm…sorry. Really, really sorry."

"No, I shouldn't make you feel bad," Ashley cried. "Your dad is serving the country in the CIA and that's a good thing. But why did Chaz have to come after you? Why did this happen?"

The candlelight flicked across Nicky's face, making his expression hard to read. A beat later, he admitted, "Come on, Ashley. That story about the CIA was a bunch of garbage, just like Jack said. Jack was right. He's always right, isn't he?"

Ashley's eyebrows rose. "I—what are you saying?"

"Don't you get it? There are no spies. I'm talking about my father's—" He swallowed and pressed his lids tight. "My father's business associates. They were like wolverines—dangerous and deadly, preying on innocent people. Or maybe not such innocent people. I just want someone to know the truth. I'm tired of the lies. I'm especially tired of lying to you."

Jack sat back on his heels. "What kind of lies?"

"Everything I ever told you. I'm sorry. But mostly I'm sorry about…" Nicky stopped, staring at them morosely as he said, "dragging you into all this. Chaz was on their payroll. It's obvious. They have connections everywhere. Even in Alaska."

"Who? Who has connections?" Jack demanded. "I don't understand."

"My dad was never with the CIA," Nicky said, keeping his eyes lowered, staring at his hands. "My dad was on the other side."

"What other side?"

"Organized crime."

Jack sucked in his breath, and even Ashley seemed shocked into silence.

Nicky muttered, "I'm sick of secrets, sick of being like that Indian woman who never got to have any friends. Because of my dad I'm alone. Always alone. But then, that's not living, is it? But telling you this—that's risky. Maybe now you hate me. You're wondering what kind of scum's been brought into your life. That's what you're thinking, isn't it?"

Sifting through it, Jack finally realized what Nicky was trying to say. Nicky's dad was a criminal. He wanted to pull away from Nicky Milano, but there was nowhere to go inside the snow cave. Organized crime. Mobsters. Scamming. Hit men. He felt his stomach turn against it all. In Jack's life, all the pieces were lined in neat, orderly rows, like books on a library shelf. His parents took care of him, he attended school and made good grades, he went to Scouts. Life stayed nice and even, and it all made sense. But this! Nicky lived in a world where people didn't think anything about killing each other for money. He felt himself shudder.

Ashley's voice had dropped to barely above a whisper. "How did this happen?"

"This is the true story," Nicky went on, his voice low, "so listen up. You might learn something. Philly's a big city, too big to fit everything under one crime family. A while back, seven years ago to be exact, my dad had a…disagreement…" he swallowed the word, "with some guys from a rival organization. They wanted him out of the way, so they tampered with the brakes on his car. Only, that morning, it was my mother who drove away in the car. End of story."

"You mean—" Ashley stuttered a little trying to say it, "Sh-she was killed in a wreck because the brakes failed? And somebody made that happen?"

"Yeah. That's what I mean." The words hung in the air. For a moment the only sound was the gas stove's quiet hissing. The candles flicked golden light on the snow walls, casting strange shadows. Jack watched the shadows morph from one shape into another. Like Nicky.

Ashley reached out as though to comfort Nicky, then pulled back. "The men who did that got arrested, I hope."

"They…disappeared."

Jack blurted, "Did your dad have them killed?"

Nicky jerked upright, his eyes flashing. "My dad is not a killer. He worked in the rackets, but he never whacked anyone."

"I didn't mean—" Jack began to protest, but Nicky talked right over him, his voice harsh. "You don't know anything—you don't know about my life. There's more than one mob in Philly and New Jersey and New York— they fight among themselves. He just got in the middle of a bad fight. He's *not* a killer!"

"I believe you," Jack assured him. "I'm sorry."

"He's *not* a killer," Nicky said again, only this time, his voice sounded empty. "My dad took paybacks from contracts he arranged—building contracts, like bridges and shopping malls and office buildings and stuff. The contractors and unions paid him, and then he passed along the money to the mob. We're talking about mucho millions of dollars."

"Whoa, that's a lot of money," Jack muttered, trying to keep from showing how shocked he felt.

"But after they killed my mom, things changed. My dad started to hate his life. He told them he wanted out. Like I said, that was seven years ago, but they wouldn't let him go."

"Why not?" Ashley said quietly.

Nicky laughed harshly. "Because in the mob, you check in, but you never check out. He was afraid for me." Nicky's eyes closed for a moment, and he took a ragged breath. "My dad said, 'The sins of the father are visited upon the son.' He was afraid they were always just one step behind, just one step. I know how bad he wanted to end that kind of life."

"So—how does Chaz fit in all of this?" Jack wanted to know.

Nicky's jaw clenched tight. "He's one of them."

"But why would he come after you? "

"Because my dad's back East testifying against the mob. They tried to get me as a hostage so they could make my dad shut up. Don't you get it? We've been in the Witness Protection Program. That's why the FBI put me into foster care under Ms. Lopez, so someone could hide me while my dad was away. She picked your family." Nicky laughed then, an angry, bitter laugh. "Turns out I wasn't safe up in the wilds of Alaska, either. If Chaz had got me into that airplane, I'm not sure which way it would have gone for me. Alive, I'd be a bargaining chip—but only for a while. Then they'd off me."

"What about us?" Ashley asked weakly.

"For you two…well, Chaz figured you'd die out here. Casualties of war. That's the part that's eating my guts right now, that because of me, you two nearly got killed. And if we don't get out of this place tomorrow, all of us still might die."

Jack and Ashley stared at each other, both of them realizing that they were lucky to be alive—for now. But what would tomorrow bring? Shaking her head, Ashley murmured, "You know what I don't get? Chaz acted like he really loved those dogs, but then he could turn around and be a cold-blooded killer."

Nicky turned his head, as if he were afraid to look

at Jack or Ashley because they might despise him now. "People do a lot of things for money, Ashley. Ask my dad." He leaned back, rubbing his shoulders against the snow wall. "I think we should get some sleep if we can. In the morning, we have to hike out of this wilderness. It could be one long, long hike."

CHAPTER TEN

It was impossible for the three of them to stretch out comfortably to sleep, but Jack pulled his knees to his chin, rested his arms across them, and then dropped his head down, down, into a strange dream world where the snow itself had teeth. Deeper into the water he swam. He saw Nicky, but this time Nicky had the gun, and he was taking Ashley to Philadelphia and Jack couldn't stop them. He ran after them and then he fell out of the plane…the ground rushed up to meet him and right before impact he jerked awake.

The pounding in his head was like a drum pulsing with every beat of his heart. He could barely open his eyes. In the light from the candle that still burned, he saw Ashley lying limp, and Nicky with his head sunk to one side, his skin the color of ashes. Jack struggled to sit up, but felt so dizzy he almost toppled over again.

He thought he might throw up. Squeezing the top of his head with his hands, he tried to get his brain working, but his thoughts were so jumbled it was as if he were still swimming up from the bottom of that pool to get some air.

Air! That was it. Straining, he peered up, looking for the ventilation hole, but he couldn't find it. It was no longer there!

Each motion made him think his head would explode. He needed air. Desperate for air! He managed to slither toward the cave entrance and began kicking the duffel bag away. Kick, kick—feet pushing toward the salvation of fresh air, his brain screaming for oxygen. When at last he broke through, he slid outside to breathe great gulps of that precious clear fresh sweet-smelling air, but only enough to clear his head, because he had to go back to rescue the other two.

First Ashley. Inside the cave, she lay unconscious, her lips a cherry red—one of the symptoms of carbon monoxide poisoning, Jack's sluggish brain remembered. Dragging his sister by her feet, he pulled her outside to safety, grabbing handfuls of snow to press against her face, hoping that would shock her awake.

"What?" she mumbled.

"Can you sit up?" Jack demanded. "Breathe! Take deep breaths."

Too groggy to fight him, Ashley did what he said. It was then Jack realized that dawn was breaking. How many hours had they lain inside that snow cave with both openings blocked—one by snow that had fallen during the night, the other by the duffel bag? While the camp stove and the candles burned oxygen out of the air—oxygen they needed to survive—the cave had filled with carbon monoxide.

"Will you keep on breathing? Promise me you'll keep taking deep breaths," Jack croaked. He hated to leave her like this, but he had to go back for Nicky.

"Get Nicky," she mumbled. "Help him."

Propping her in a sitting position against the side of the snow cave, he shouted, "Remember to breathe!" and climbed again into the cave.

Nicky looked dead. For a terrifying moment, Jack thought he was too late. He quickly pulled off his glove; with a shaking hand, he pressing his fingers against Nicky's neck and felt a faint pulse, as faint as a butterfly's wing. Nicky was alive, but maybe not for long.

Because Nicky was much bigger and heavier than Ashley, getting him out wouldn't be as easy. Jack hesitated, wondering how to move him. Jack's head still throbbed, but at least his mind became somewhat lucid again. He maneuvered himself to grip Nicky from behind, circling his arms around Nicky's chest as if they were on a toboggan together. He'd try to slide him through the entryway.

Nicky's knees crumpled awkwardly as Jack tugged and pulled and grunted with the effort. It wasn't going to work. He'd have to get out of the cave himself, then grab Nicky by his feet, pulling dead weight. Panting hard, struggling for what seemed like hours but was no more than a few minutes, Jack finally got him out.

By the time Nicky was stretched out on the ground, Ashley had begun to talk rationally again. She crawled on her knees to Nicky, leaned over him, and cupped his face in her hands, calling, "Nicky, Nicky! Wake up. Please, Nicky, wake up and talk to me. You need to breathe!"

Guilt washed over Jack as powerfully as waves of nausea. He should have known what might happen. Why had he blocked that front entrance! He knew ventilation required a flow-through. Why hadn't he at least dug a second ventilation hole? Nicky had said Jack was always right—what a joke! He'd almost gotten the three of them killed!

Slumping onto the snow, lying on his back, he stared up at the sky, where the sun had just risen over the peak, so bright in the clear cold air that it almost blinded him. Branches spread above him like Irish lace, and in the very top of them he could see the remains of a nest. It was peaceful here, quiet, like a cemetery. Twice in the past 24 hours they'd barely cheated death. They were still stranded in Denali in freezing temperatures miles from help and food. How many more times could they dodge a bullet? Was this their day to die?

His head not only throbbed, it buzzed. Buzzed like a mosquito, then more like a bee, then louder, like a wasp. With his eyes squeezed almost shut, because the light from the sun was so dazzling, he peered upward and saw motion. Not an insect, an airplane!

"Ashley!" he yelled, jumping up and then almost falling down again because he was still dizzy. "Look up there! We're rescued!"

"Can they see us?" she asked.

He didn't know if they could. None of them wore bright colors—their parkas and ski pants would look as drab against the snow as tree shadows. "Wave your arms!" he told her. "Do what I tell you. Wave your arms!"

Ashley ignored him. Instead, she unzipped the pocket in her parka and took out a folding comb.

A comb! "What are you doing?" he hollered.

Still not answering, she unfolded the comb, which had a small mirror in the handle. Holding up the mirror to catch the sun's strong rays, she angled it back and forth. "I'm sending a signal," she told him. "They'll notice the flash."

Jack almost laughed out loud. Trust Ashley to come up with the simplest, best solution.

The plane dropped lower in the morning sky, circled once, and buzzed them.

They'd been seen!

#

The three of them lounged in the Denali ranger's home, Jack in a large, overstuffed chair, sipping a cup of hot cocoa next to a cheerful fire. Everything in the room had been decorated in earthen hues, as though the owners had tried to package Denali's wild outdoors. Plants sprouted from every corner with broad, emerald hands that seemed to reach out, open palmed, toward furniture made from walnut and pine. The one burst of bright color came from a wall covered with photographs of the park's wildflowers: yellow Alaska poppies, pink fireweed, purple forget-me-nots, bluebells, arctic daisies, and an ivory field of cotton grass that stretched across a wide meadow.

"I'll never understand why they call such a pretty flower fireweed," Ashley said. She was standing next to the wall with the picture of the pink flowers, her finger tracing the petals that burst from the stalk.

"Because those are the flowers that pull through after a fire," Jack answered. "Their roots go deep. That's how they are able to survive."

Nicky sat nestled into a recliner close to the fireplace, wiggling his toes inside thick wool socks. At his side sat a popcorn bowl holding a few unpopped kernels and next to that was a half-filled glass of soda. To Jack, Nicky looked perfectly content. Webbing his fingers behind his head, Nicky stretched lazily, then said, "Survivors, huh? Kind of like us."

"Like us, for sure," Ashley echoed. She went over to his side, hovering for a moment before asking, "Do you need anything, Nicky?" When she picked up the empty metal bowl the kernels rattled across the bottom, creating a sound like rain. "Want more popcorn?"

Jack put down his book and frowned. "Give me a break, Ashley. I mean, you haven't asked if *I* need anything, and you've already brought Nicky one bowl of popcorn. He's not an invalid."

"I appreciate your sister's very kind hospitality," Nicky drawled.

Jack countered, "You appreciate my sister waiting on you hand and foot."

Nicky wiggled his eyebrows. "Maybe she respects the fact that I dug out most of the snow cave."

"You did not—we did that together. Besides, I'm the one who designed it. And I kicked the wolverine."

"I scared it away with my shovel."

"Guys!" Ashley cried, stomping her foot so hard her curls jiggled. *"I'm* the one who signaled the plane and got us rescued. You don't hear me bragging. You two have got to quit fighting!"

Snickering, Jack ducked his head and retreated once again behind his book. "We're not fighting," he told her.

"Nah, we're just playing with you," Nicky agreed. He picked up his glass and rattled the ice cubes. "But I *would* like more Coke."

"That's great," Ashley answered, smiling sweetly. "Get it yourself." Sighing, she dropped onto the sofa and declared, "Like I said before, guys are so dumb!" But she couldn't suppress the lilt in her voice when she said it, because the three of them had been baiting and picking since they'd arrived yesterday morning. It felt good to tease. Normal. As if their close brush with death hadn't really happened.

Olivia's voice chattered in the background, then Jack heard her hang up the phone. A moment later, she poked her head in from the kitchen. "You kids OK in there?" she asked for the hundredth time.

"We're fine," Jack called back. "Who was that on the phone?"

"Park headquarters." She had a kitchen towel in her hand, which she slung over her shoulder. Olivia wore a green jogging suit, the kind that was lined inside, with a green turtleneck underneath and green slipper socks. That morning, when she asked Jack how she looked, he told her she looked like a stalk of asparagus. In reply she told him he was grounded for life. She must have forgiven him, because now she settled down on the footstool next to Jack and said, "You're never going to believe this! The lab called with their report, and I was right. I figured out how Chaz killed the wolverines."

"What?" Ashley asked, wide-eyed. "How?"

"He drowned them."

"Drowned them?" Jack shuddered. The good mood he'd been enjoying suddenly evaporated as he thought of the animals' final moments.

"I would never have figured it out if you kids hadn't told me exactly what Chaz said. He was right—I was stumped. No poison, no disease, no obvious sign of trauma. But I decided to check the tissue itself under a microscope, and lo and behold, I discovered ice crystals in the lungs. Those animals weren't within a mile of water, so I never would have looked for that."

"How…" Jack started to ask.

"The police found wire cages in his home. He must have lowered the cages into water while the wolverines were inside."

"Oh."

Olivia shook her head. "I should have known something was wrong with Chaz. I wondered about what he said just before he took you away on his sled—that he couldn't tell the difference between male and female wolverines. I thought that was really strange since the males are so much bigger. It crossed my mind that if he was such a wolverine lover, he should have known that. I can't help but think that if only I'd been more suspicious.…"

"It's not your fault, Mom," Jack told her. "He was a sick man."

"Not sick," Nicky said. "Greedy."

"You're right, Nicky," Olivia agreed softly. "He was sick with greed."

Just then the front door rattled open, and Steven ushered in a small woman wearing a gray national park uniform. A stiff felt hat was perched on the ranger's head, its broad rim casting a shadow over her eyes. Her olive jacket was unzipped, revealing a thick belt that had real bullets in it. Glossy brown hair had been secured at the nape of her neck with a plastic clip. When she took off her coat, Jack saw her gold badge. It read, "Annalie Wright."

"Olivia, kids," Steven called, shrugging off his coat. "I'd like to introduce you to Annalie. She's one of the law enforcement rangers assigned to the case."

Olivia stood, wiping her hands on the towel before flinging it over her shoulder again. "Pleased to meet you," she said, giving Annalie a firm handshake. "Let me take your jacket."

"Thanks," Annalie said, taking off her hat. When they'd settled into the living room, Annalie's smile faded. Jack could tell that whatever she was about to say was serious. For a moment they all sat there, waiting, while Annalie smoothed the pleat on her pant leg.

"Well, we found Chaz." She cleared her throat and glanced at the floor, before raising her eyes once again to rest on Nicky's. "He was buried about 50 yards from the sled, under 8 feet of snow. He's dead, Nicky. He won't be bothering you anymore."

Nicky said nothing. The room was suddenly silent.

Jack took a breath. That's what he'd expected, but it still felt strange to hear it. Right then, the biggest feeling he had was relief, which was a strange emotion considering a man was dead.

"So, what about me?" Nicky asked slowly. "Am I OK? I mean, am I safe now?"

"Uh…." She cleared her throat again. "I can't really answer that, Nicky, but I do have some good news for you. A surprise, really."

"A great surprise!" Steven agreed, pulling himself up out of the chair. And then, loudly, he called, "Paul, come on in!"

CHAPTER ELEVEN

Who was Paul, Jack wondered, but then Nicky was jumping up yelling, "Dad! What are you doing here?" A tall, thin man strode forward, his arms outstretched. Father and son gripped each other tightly, so tight Jack could see muscles bulge from the base of Nicky's neck like thin ropes. Two other men waited just outside the door in the shadows, both wearing long, dark over-coats that looked out of place in Denali, where every-one else wore parkas. The men's faces bore no expressions at all.

"I'm here, Son," Paul said, his voice husky. "I'm through testifying. I'm—I'm so sorry I put you in so much danger." His dark eyes filmed with tears as he looked around the room at the others and said, "I apol-ogize to you all, from the very bottom of my heart, for endangering the lives of these children." Since emotion seemed to overcome him, Jack wondered if everyone else should leave the room so Nicky and his father could have some privacy.

"Dad, we're *fine*," Nicky told him eagerly, his words muffled by his father's deep embrace. When he pried free, he went to where Ashley stood, took her hand in his and said, "Ashley, I want you to meet my father. Dad, this is Ashley."

"Hi," Ashley said shyly. She gave a tiny wave, and Paul smiled at her.

Then, almost as an afterthought, Nicky added, "Oh, and this is Steven and Olivia Landon, and their son, Jack. Olivia is like, this animal guru, and she can take you all around Denali and tell you anything you want to know about the animals."

Olivia reached out to take Paul's hand. "I think that's a *slight* exaggeration. But welcome to Denali."

"And Steven is a photographer. When we're back in Jackson Hole, you'll get to see some of his pictures—they're hanging in a gallery. And this is Jack. He's the one who knew all about the snow cave—did anyone tell you about the snow cave we were in, Dad? We would have frozen to death for sure if Jack hadn't known how to build it."

"Yeah, but we also got pretty sick from the carbon monoxide poisoning," Jack added modestly. He didn't want to take too much credit—not after he'd almost killed them.

Paul looked different from what Jack had expected. Even though his clothes seemed expensive, his face was worn down and used up, as if life had weighed hard on him. Jack had imagined anyone working for the mob would have a broad barrel chest and a neck as thick as a tree trunk, but maybe he'd been watching too many crime shows on TV. He'd also expected to be afraid of this man, this former criminal. Yet Paul just appeared like any other father who might have shown up at his son's soccer practice in Jackson Hole. Maybe, Jack decided, that was even more frightening.

Nicky's father shifted uncomfortably when the two men in overcoats cleared their throats. His eyes flicked over to where the men stood, and the men gave back the barest nod. Nicky was in the middle of telling about the wolverine breaking into the snow cave when Paul interrupted quietly with, "Son, we have to go."

Nicky froze. "What do you mean 'go?' You mean go *now?*"

Paul nodded slowly.

"Are we going home to Jackson Hole?"

With a smile that seemed like more of a grimace, Paul said, "No, we're going to a new place. It'll be great. We'll be out in the country, with plenty of open space. This time I think you'll be able to have that horse I promised you. You'd like that, wouldn't you?"

"But I want to stay in Jackson Hole," Nicky answered firmly. "I have friends now. Jack and Ashley."

"I know, and I understand, but we can't go back."

"Dad, no!"

"Listen to me and try to understand. Chaz—that guy who took you—he was a hit man. Trust me, there are more where he came from. There are always more."

"But—"

"Starting over's the only way. It's dangerous for us if we don't do that."

"So we're leaving," Nicky said with resignation. "When?"

"Right away."

Nicky sagged. He looked over at Ashley. As if on cue, Olivia and Steven got up quietly, and Olivia said, "I'll make some coffee. Would you like to join us for a cup, Annalie?"

Annalie slapped her thighs and stood, then walked toward the door. "How about you two fellows coming into the kitchen and joining us?" she suggested. "You have time for a cup of coffee, don't you?"

The men looked at each other, then nodded. "Sure, we can do that," one of them said. "Just a cup, though. We're on a tight schedule."

They accompanied Annalie to the kitchen. When Jack and Ashley started to follow the group as well, Nicky stopped them. "No, I want you guys to stay here with me. If this has gotta be good-bye, I don't want to waste a minute."

"Sure," Jack told him. "We'll stay if you want us to."

He felt awkward as he and Ashley perched on the edge of the sofa. Paul dropped down onto an overstuffed chair and dangled his thin hands between his knees, moving his fingers nervously as if he were used to holding a cigarette. Nicky sat in a chair directly across from his father.

It took Paul a moment to speak. "Do they understand about me?" he asked, pointing a finger toward Ashley and Jack.

"Enough." Nicky's tone made no apologies. "I've never told anyone before, Dad. But this was different. I wanted them to know who I was."

"Of course. It's all right. I'm just embarrassed." Paul blinked hard. "It's difficult to admit how much I've messed up my life. I've had to come to grips with that these past few months. And as bad as that was, the worst part is knowing that I've hurt my own child. You're all I've got left, Son."

Quietly, Nicky answered, "You're all I've got, too."

His father took a deep, wavering breath. "I'm going to promise you something, Nicky, and it's a promise I'm going to keep. From now on things are going to be different. I've left that old life for good. Witness Protection's giving me a new identity, and I'm going to make my fresh start count. You have my word."

"I know, Dad, and that's great, but—" he dropped his head into his hands and rubbed his temples. When he looked up, he seemed grim. "The problem is, when you trade in your old life, you trade in mine, too. I was just getting into a new life of my own, and now you're taking it way from me. It's not fair."

Jack noticed the dark roots growing in Nicky's hair. Maybe in his next home he wouldn't have to dye it. Maybe he wouldn't have to lie anymore. Nicky and his dad could start over, with crisp new government-issued identities. But once your life was erased, what was left? Who did you become? Did you get to choose?

"Son, I'll spend what's left of my days trying to make this up to you. If I could change the past I'd do it, but now all I can do is play out the hand I've been dealt. My time here in Denali is already up. We have to go."

Nicky didn't answer. He stared at the carpet.

"Do you get what I'm telling you?"

After a moment, Nicky nodded.

"All right then. I'm guessing you want to say your good-byes in private. I can give you that much."

A flush crept up Nicky's cheeks.

"So I'll go into the kitchen with the others." When Paul stood, he let his hand linger for a moment on the top of Nicky's head. "Five minutes, and then we'll leave. I'm—I'm sorry." Moving quickly, he made his way to the kitchen.

Silence seemed to fill the room, and Jack searched his mind for something to say. Nicky kept his head bowed, and when he finally spoke it was as if he were talking to the floor. "So I guess I'm leaving," he finally said. His voice was flat.

Ashley settled onto the floor next to the chair where Nicky sat. "Can you write me?" she asked him.

"I don't think so. It's not allowed."

"Oh." She began to pick up popcorn kernels that had fallen onto the carpet, throwing them one by one into the fireplace.

"It's not fair!" Nicky shouted, finally raising his head. "I've never had a good friend—friends—like you guys. I mean, you know *everything* about me, and you don't hate me. I really appreciate that. We've been through a lot together."

"Yeah," Jack agreed heartily. "We sure have."

"Now I know never to make a snow cave without lots of ventilation. Although, with my luck we'll end up in Arizona so I'll never get to use that piece of information again." He laughed, but it wasn't a happy sound. "Look, the thing is—the thing is," he started again, "I'm gonna call you guys someday. In a couple of years," he promised, glancing at Ashley, "you can count on me showing up. Because good friends are hard to find. You know?"

"I know," she answered softly. "But you're like the fireweed, Nicky. No matter what, you'll survive."

"Thanks, Ashley." Slowly, Nicky stood. "Well, I know the drill. I have to go pack now."

"Need any help?" Jack volunteered.

Nicky just shook his head. "I've learned to travel light. Seems I'm always going somewhere."

It was harder than Jack expected to see him go. He'd stood next to Ashley, waving at the shiny black Jeep as it drove away with the shadow men in front, Paul and Nicky in the back. They waved until the car disappeared beyond a bend in the road, swallowed by the spruce trees, and Ashley kept waving, even though there was nothing but the wind blowing back through the bare branches as if it were heaving a sigh. Jack grabbed the neck of his sweatshirt and pulled it tight. Neither of them had a coat on. He could feel his sister shiver.

"Well, there goes your first boyfriend."

"He was *not* my boyfriend!" She punched his arm hard enough that it stung. "I'm only 11."

"Eleven and *half!*"

"Whatever. Nicky's just a friend. A really *good* friend." She looked wistfully into the distance.

"It's really strange to think about how he'll change into somebody else. Can you imagine how it would be to wake up with a new name and a new life? Weird!"

Ashley hugged her sides tight. "I guess. But in a way, we change all the time, every day. I mean, look at us. We're growing up. I'm different than I was yesterday, and I bet I'll feel different tomorrow. It's just the way things are."

As Jack turned this thought over he realized what his sister said was true. Trying to stop life would be like trying to hold on to the northern lights—it couldn't be done. But he didn't have to like it.

"Remember, change is a good thing, Jack."

"Yeah, I know. As long as it doesn't come too fast." He grabbed Ashley by the elbow. "Come on, we'd better get inside before you freeze to death."

But his sister resisted his pull. "Nicky said he'd come back in a couple years. Do you think he'll really do it?"

Jack paused. "If he does, I'll be waiting for him."

"We *both* will," Ashley replied, smiling.

AFTERWORD

As Jack, Ashley, and Nicky learned from their adventure in Denali National Park and Preserve, the wilderness can be a dangerous place. Just as animals that live in Denali must find ways to adapt to the extreme conditions in order to survive, people who visit the park must be aware of the challenges they might encounter and be prepared to deal with them.

The powerfully built wolverine, featured in the story, is an example of an animal that is well suited for surviving in this environment. Its body structure and posture allow it to travel through deep snow. With its strong teeth, it can forage on the bones and frozen meat of dead animals. Wolverines sometimes go after live animals, too, even large ones such as moose or caribou when they get caught in deep snow. Wolverines are so ferocious that they've been known to scare a grizzly bear away from its own kill! Since the chances of encountering a wolverine are slight because of the animal's secretive behavior, it's a rare and exciting treat to actually see one in the wild, as Jack, Ashley, and Nicky did. Considering how fierce these animals can be, the three kids were lucky to escape without a scratch when they came face to face with the wolverine that entered their snow cave.

Jack's ability to keep a rational mind and not panic in the face of danger meant the difference between life and death for the three kids. He was able to avoid catastrophe by drawing on the survival skills he acquired as an Eagle Scout. Jack knew that long exposure in the extreme cold would eventually cause their body temperatures to drop. He also knew that this condition, known as hypothermia, could interfere with their ability to think clearly and could even kill them. By using his knowledge and staying calm, he was able to convince Ashley and Nicky that building a snow cave was necessary for their survival.

He relied on his scouting experience to build a very well constructed snow cave, but he made one serious mistake. When he blocked the entrance of the cave with the duffel bag after the encounter with the wolverine, he forgot to make new holes for ventilation. Air circulation is crucial. After the candles and camp stove used up the cave's oxygen because the hole in the roof had become blocked by snow, Jack, Ashley, and Nicky were overcome by carbon monoxide. Jack's error nearly cost them their lives.

Denali isn't the only national park where sound knowledge and good judgment play important roles in survival. While the conditions in Denali are extremely severe for a large part of the year, environmental conditions in the lower 48 states can also be hazardous. For example, heat exhaustion and dehydration in southern environments—Death Valley, for instance—also can be fatal.

Anyone who participates in wilderness recreational activities should research the area to be visited. Read about environmental conditions that may be encountered, obtain maps of the area, know how to use a compass or GPS (global positioning system) device, and talk to park rangers or other experts in the area. Always plan properly for the trip. Determine the equipment you'll need to stay safe and comfortable, learn first-aid skills, and study the potential risks you may encounter during your visit.

Find out the best way to communicate. Cell phones may not work and two-way radios may not have the range needed to get help if you are faced with a serious situation. Establish a detailed itinerary that includes an emergency contact, and leave it with someone who will know whom to call if you're overdue from your trek.

Park rangers will be glad to help you plan your adventure. They can tell you how to cross rivers or streams, and what to do when you encounter a potentially dangerous animal such as grizzly bear or a cow moose with a calf. They can warn you about possible avalanche danger, or about rapidly changing weather conditions that indicate a developing storm. With proper planning and preparation, your wilderness adventure will be enjoyable, rewarding, and a whole lot safer.

Diane Brown
Communication Center Manager
Denali National Park and Preserve

DON'T MISS—

WOLF STALKER
MYSTERY #1
Fast-paced adventure has the Landons on the trail
of a wounded wolf in Yellowstone National Park.

CLIFF-HANGER
MYSTERY #2
Jack's desire to help the headstrong Lucky Deal
brings him face-to-face with a hungry cougar in
Mesa Verde National Park.

DEADLY WATERS
MYSTERY #3
Jack and Ashley's efforts to save an injured manatee
involve them in a thrilling chase through the Everglades.

RAGE OF FIRE
MYSTERY #4
In this tale of myth and mystery, a Vietnamese orphan
named Danny leads Ashley and Jack into a steaming
crater in Hawaii Volcanoes National Park.

THE HUNTED
MYSTERY #5
While attempting to help a young Mexican runaway, Jack
and Ashley flee for their lives from an enraged mother
grizzly in Glacier National Park.

GHOST HORSES
MYSTERY #6
Life-threatening accidents plague the Landons as they
investigate the mysterious deaths of some white mustangs
on a trip to Zion National Park.

OVER THE EDGE
MYSTERY #7
Jack relies on high-tech cyber skills to find out who is threatening his mother after she broadcasts her plan to save the condors in Grand Canyon National Park.

VALLEY OF DEATH
MYSTERY #8
A showdown with Ashley's kidnappers leads the Landons to a missile testing ground and the key to what's killing the desert bighorn sheep in Death Valley National Park.

ESCAPE FROM FEAR
MYSTERY #9
On a trip to Virgin Islands National Park to study sea turtles and coral reefs, the Landons become entangled in a teenage boy's desperate efforts to save the mysterious Cimmaron.

OUT OF THE DEEP
MYSTERY #10
A baby humpback whale is the latest marine mammal to strand along the rocky shores of Acadia National Park, and the race is on to figure out what's causing the strange behavior before more lives are endangered.

RUNNING SCARED
MYSTERY #11
While lost in a cave in Carlsbad Caverns National Park, the Landon kids stumble on to some cave robbers and uncover a clue that helps explain the park's dwindling bat population.

To read samples from these mysteries,
go to Gloria Skurzynski's Web site:
http://gloriabooks.com/national.html

ABOUT THE AUTHORS

An award-winning mystery writer and an award-winning science writer—who are also mother and daughter—are working together on Mysteries in Our National Parks!

Alane (Lanie) Ferguson's first mystery, *Show Me the Evidence,* won the Edgar Award, given by the Mystery Writers of America.

Gloria Skurzynski's *Almost the Real Thing* won the American Institute of Physics Science Writing Award.

Lanie lives in Elizabeth, Colorado. Gloria lives in Boise, Idaho. To work together on a novel, they connect by phone, fax, and e-mail and "often forget which one of us wrote a particular line."

Gloria's e-mail: gloriabooks@qwest.net
Her Web site: http://gloriabooks.com
Lanie's e-mail: aferguson@sprynet.com
Her Web site: http://alaneferguson.com